CrossStar:
Secrets of Elizabeth

Natasha Levinski

AuthorHouse™
1663 Liberty Drive
Bloomington, IN 47403
www.authorhouse.com
Phone: 1-800-839-8640

© 2010 Natasha Levinski. All rights reserved.

No part of this book may be reproduced, stored in a retrieval system, or transmitted by any means without the written permission of the author.

First published by AuthorHouse 12/13/2010

ISBN: 978-1-4520-9627-8 (e)
ISBN: 978-1-4520-9626-1 (sc)

Printed in the United States of America

Certain stock imagery © Thinkstock.

This book is printed on acid-free paper.

Because of the dynamic nature of the Internet, any Web addresses or links contained in this book may have changed since publication and may no longer be valid. The views expressed in this work are solely those of the author and do not necessarily reflect the views of the publisher, and the publisher hereby disclaims any responsibility for them.

To my grandfather,
You're my brother's guardian angel.
Every time he's about to hurt himself you say 'stupid kid' and pluck him out of danger.
Thank you.

Elyon

I still didn't know why I was here. The dark scariness of this new dimension broke all the laws I've known. Every thing I've learned and everything I've loved. I have had to give up so many things that would have needed to be there in my life. All those experiences that came with growing, the good and the bad.

Have you ever noticed what is good for you might be bad for some one else? For instance people who are on the side of light hate darkness. To them, it's a vine or disease that creeps up their legs then slowly up their body. For people on the side of darkness, light is blinding, it bends their senses in a way that is unruly and completely vile.

What I'm trying to get at here is that everyone is on the same side, everyone wants what's 'good' for their team, only if others understood…

Prologue:
The Beginning

Elizabeth

"Mom's going to bring us to Wonderland tomorrow, aren't you excited?" Ely asked as she jumped up and down on the rickety bridge.

"Yay," Antoinette cheered as she slid down a slide.

"So, I went to a *ball* the other night!" I stuck out my tongue as I swung higher and higher on the swings. When I was four I was always scared of heights but now that I'm a whole two years older they're no problem.

"Liz, why do you have to go and say those things?" Ely stomped her foot and slipped. She rubbed away at a scratch and turned to look at me.

"Because the faery place is *way* more fun than stupid Weston." I crossed my arms in front of my chest.

"I'm telling mom you *swore*, Elizabeth!" she gasped clasping her hand around her mouth. She jumped off

Natasha Levinski

the bridge and ran out of the playground towards our house.

"Don't! I didn't mean it!" I yelled after her but she was already a block away.

Chapter 1

The Wrong Life at the Wrong Time
Elyon

I WAS A DEPRESSED TYPE of girl, very hard headed, arrogant and maybe forceful at times.

It all began a few days ago. I found myself in what I believed to be the Faery world. I didn't get there on my own, but somehow they had brought me here.

I was frightened of what stood before me. Scared half to death. The horrible things that I couldn't say in my own words, were actually alive *in front* of me. They were creatures and the most vile and cruel things ever. Now my life had opened a door and welcomed them in.

I was standing in front of 10 creatures. The creature in the center was really making it hard not to stare. 'It' had no head but a body and legs; its eyes were on its chest plate and mouth, below its diaphragm. And believe it or not, this was the KING. Not of where you and I live on Earth but in NorthStar, another dimension between space itself.

Beside the King, the Queen tapped her long ice like nails on the desk she sat at.

She looked 'a little' more normal than her partner. At least her body was the same as a human woman's, maybe a little taller. But her skin was Caribbean blue and her hair was Arctic white. Her eyes were as black as the darkest black hole in the universe. She was frightening in the sense that she had power, while the King's appearance was frightening, if you know what I mean. The other eight were all dressed in black and looked human enough except for the wings out of their backs.

Your mother or father must have told you a fairy tale once in your life. Well, you probably heard that the fairies had fairy wings, all pretty and pointy, kind of like butterfly wings. But the wings I saw looked like wings of a crow, but translucent. They were horrible looking and sent the message that even the slightest touch would cause a gash through your hand.

"Elyon! You are here under circumstances that you must not know of!" said the King.

I looked at the King who had roared at me so loudly that I shook.

"Know what?" I asked, I think my question was more for my pleasure than as an answer to his question. A better reason was because I was trying to hide my fright.

"Do you know of the circumstance you are not supposed to know?" he asked. He was so confusing that I was holding back really hard from laughing... and shaking.

"Know of what circumstances?"

"The circumstances of your sister!" he screamed at the top of his lungs. I heard a gasp around the coliseum.

"No, no *I didn't*." I said with a sinister look, but deep inside something cracked, like my awkwardly mended heart shattering into millions of pieces.

"Now you are guilty of trickery!" bellowed the King.

"Now we're in court?" I asked smiling.

"ELYON! I banish you from NorthStar!" In that instant I was gone from the land of Fey and back home.

I've had some hints throughout my life about the Fey. When I was a child I had a sister, a twin sister. Her name was Elizabeth. Now, Elizabeth was different, she would talk about another world all the time, and about faeries. Not F-A-I-R-Y, but F-A-E-R-Y. Do you see the difference?

She would always talk about her adventures in the park but I never believed her. My mother didn't like Elizabeth's imagination and one night Elizabeth didn't come back from the park. I would wait everyday on the swing set. But she never came back.

The second hint was Seth; well I didn't know his name before, when I was a child. But all those days when I would wait for Elizabeth at the swings, in the open swing next to me sat Seth, brilliantly pale skin and charcoal hair. He just sat there, looking at me, never really saying anything until I was totally struck with depression, then he became one of my best friends.

The final hint was that I have always sensed something other than the things around me. As if another living being was there beside me. Or many have been beside me. I've always felt another breeze, breath, upon me. The Fey.

*

I walked down Little Avenue and turned the corner of a stone wall towards my apartment.

I trudged in the rain puddles and wet grass not thinking about anything in particular.

"Hey, Elyon!" I heard a familiar voice call. I turned around to see Charlie, Leslie and Mandy leaning against the river wall.

I wondered at first why they were out so late but it was probably only eight pm. You see, Fey had a different time set than we have. If I was let's say stuck there for ten days it would only be a day here. You can do the math if you want to figure out the formula and get all technical by yourself. Hey, it's Spring Break for me.

I walked towards them, they were my school friends. We hung out sometimes but secretly I didn't like them at all. They didn't even make me happy; they probably encouraged this whole depression thing if I thought about it.

"Slugger, want to hang out tonight? Party at Delaine's, her beau just bought a new place, you're invited." Charlie said, taking out an energy drink from her book bag.

"I'm not in the mood." I said about to turn around.

"Oh yeah, you and Del-Z got in a fight." Leslie said, making my nerves tight.

I *hated* Leslie and everyone knew that. She was Charlie's cousin so *obviously* she had to be in our group.

"No Slie," I clenched my fists together, "*that* was Mandy here. I don't do the fight thing."

"Oh." she said backing down. No matter how much Slie, Leslie (the main reason why Charlie and our group is cool is because of the nicknames we give people, it kind of helps people figure out their stereotype, says Charlie), tried to get on my nerves she knew how much I over ruled her. She was a year younger than me, which made a *huge* difference.

Charlie was about to say something but Mandy slipped and she rushed to help her.

"Bye, Slugger." Charlie said as I waved good bye.

I walked through my main entrance, struggling to get my keys to my apartment out from my bag. Once I finally retrieved the keychain of the most random things I walked up the metal stairs to my room.

"How did it go?" the voice scared me and I turned. But nobody was there. I looked around scanning the foyer but I couldn't see a single soul.

"Up here." The voice called. I looked up and on the bench of the top floor window sat Seth, he had grown since I was a little kid and now looked handsome, but not my type. I just kept on staring until he jumped down, creating quite a shock through me, he jumped five floors! I probably let out a shrill scream but I can't remember it at all.

"Hello Elyon." He said giving me his usual half-smile. He was so perfect he was frightening, just like NorthStar; perfection wrapped in a frightening box. "How did the council seem?" he was looking for an answer but I was incapable of uttering words.

"I'm not allowed there." the sentence didn't sound right, my voice cracked halfway through it and I felt embarrassed for some reason.

"How was the king?" Seth pressed.

"Frightening. Seth what-"

"No, Elyon." He whispered. "Not here." He took my arm and brought me up to my room. He opened the locked door and walked in. I sighed then followed, I searched my cluttered bag for no reason.

"Elyon, NorthStar isn't for the faint of heart, which is why most of us move to CrossStar, it's more like Smallville compared to Toronto." He took my hand and led me to my retro couch which was shaped like lips, how irrelevant. I knew my friends loved it but Seth hated the garage sale couch with a passion.

"Elyon!" Seth barked. I whipped my head around to face him.

"Seth, this isn't a good time, I'm scared of NorthStar, alright! I'm scared that all the things my sister used to talk about are true, even the scary things about CrossStar! How would you feel if your crazy sister's dreams started coming true, and you were in the middle of it all?"

"CrossStar isn't scum like NorthStar!"

"My sister said-"

"Your sister was one of them!" there was silence for a while. Then Seth's pearl skin skimmed across my face and wiped a tear droplet from my eye before it fell down my cheek. "Sorry." He mumbled. "You really cared for her. You must miss her…" Seth looked away.

"We have to go back; you have to come to CrossStar." My pulse began to quicken and my palms began to sweat. I remembered exactly what Elizabeth had said about CrossStar:

"…I asked the Queen why, she said 'because they hated NorthStars, they wanted to rule the realm, takeover.' I believe her; I have never been to CrossStar though, people say its streets are filled with garbage and people close their shutters to protect themselves from the animals and rats. It doesn't sound very nice. We must not go to CrossStar Elyon, when you come, do not go there. You may never need to come, but if that one day comes I will send a guard to protect you, when I'm gone or when I'm queen."

She was right and wrong. Right as in Seth is here, here to protect me. Wrong as in I have already been there and I am going to CrossStar.

"Do you want some Fettuccini Alfredo; I can make it in a second." Seth asked as he rummaged through my small kitchen cabinets.

"That'd be great, Seth." I said while lying on my 'hot lips' couch. A headache had come randomly from nowhere and I felt sick to my stomach.

"Mushroom or original?" he asked showing the boxes.

"Original. Why did I even buy mushroom?" I asked grabbing the box of noodle mix away from him.

"Probably Antoinette, you know how much she *loves* mushrooms." He shrugged.

"Yeah but she hasn't lived here since we were both little kids." I said referring to a friend who was raised with me, since she was an orphan.

"I guess your mother never cleaned out the cupboards." He said turning on the stove and pouring a half cup of milk into a pot.

"I guess…" I trailed off. I walked to the two-chaired kitchen bar. I had lived in this apartment my whole life and when my mother moved out of it I decided to keep it. She said I could live alone for a while as long as I keep up with the rent.

"So… how's that song you're writing? Is it coming along?" Seth asked gesturing towards my half open guitar case.

"Yeah, it's fine." I shrugged. Knowing where this conversation was going.

"Can you sing it for me?" he asked smiling.

"Aww, not today, Seth, I'm not in the mood." I looked away from him; I knew he was trying to suck me into it, probably using the puppy dog face.

"Come on, it was going *really* well." He pressed; I could hear his footsteps coming towards me.

"No, the verses aren't even finished yet and mainly I have a suckish singing voice." I rolled my eyes at the ground trying not to make eye contact.

I felt his cold hands rub against my shoulders and my breath caught. I could feel his warm breath against my ear and everything in my body tingled.

CrossStar: Secrets of Elizabeth

"Please, for me." He whispered; I finally turned my head to him so we were face to face. My breath caught again as I realized how close we were.

"Fine," I said as I gulped. "As long as you back away." I pushed him away trying to breathe.

We *weren't* together; it would be weird if we were. He practically *lived* at my place and only slept at his ginormous mansion on the same street as Antoinette. But we weren't a couple; I dated other guys but I *was* currently single… I wiped that thought out of my head quickly before Seth could understand.

"Sorry." He said into his collar. I walked into my room and retrieved my lyrics and then re-entered the living room, grabbing my guitar.

I first tuned a few strings which were completely out of wack and then practiced the tune.

"Remind me what the songs about again," Seth relaxed on one of the armchairs.

"I wrote it to this guy who I like who *totally* doesn't know I exist." I said while having my pick in my mouth, so my words were slurred and spit flew out of my mouth at each word.

"I know how that feels." Seth mumbled; I looked up at him.

"You like a faery chick? Tell me what her name is! How long have you liked her?" I interrogated, completely excited at the fact that *maybe* Seth has finally found the girl for him; which leaves loads off of *my* shoulders.

"I'm not one of your friends at a thirteen year olds sleepover." Seth laughed and I did too.

"She's not a faery, just to tell you up front." He said

giving me one of his embarrassed smiles I always loved to tease him about.

"Ooh! Is she like a witch or something, or maybe some sort of princess?" I asked completely ecstatic.

"You could say that." He nodded but it wasn't a complete yes nod more like a 'you're close' nod.

"Ok, I'm sorry but that was *way* too much girly for me in one day, thank you very much." I said ending Seth's girlfriend info hunt.

"Thank, god." He laughed. "Okay sorry back to your song."

"I'm warning you, you've already heard me sing so if I make you go deaf I'm not paying your hospital bill."

"You're not *that* bad of a singer, Ely." He said sitting beside me.

"Okay so this song is a duet, so if you don't mind…" I trailed my sentence and looked at Seth.

"Sure whatever, but you thought *you* couldn't sing, wait until you hear *me*."

He grabbed the lyrics sheet and held it out for both of us. I started the tune by humming and then started the guitar intro. I silently gestured to Seth that I go first and then he does, he nodded and I started to sing…

"You should be sorry, you forgot me,
It's all you're fault, don't blame it on me.
You're so stupid, you let me down,
Who knew your evil would stay around, no.
You're so sad; you think you got me mad,
I'm so, I don't know I just lost control I just lost control."

I started playing the chorus and he nodded remembering it. When I gave him the signal he started singing in a beautiful voice:

*"I'm so slow, how could I not know,
Our feelings would continue to grow.
I'm so blue, I always think of you,
You're always on my mind; I don't know what to do.
Don't know what to prove.
I'm so apologetic, I'm pathetic,
I'm so, I don't know, I just lost control, I just lost control."*

Seth stopped singing and I stopped playing guitar. He motioned me to continue the chorus. But I just stared at him in awe.

When he sung, it sounded perfect. The song made so much more sense with him in it. But I didn't know what that meant. It was like some dream that is lost when you're just about to tell someone.

"Elyon, chorus…" Seth gestured. I looked down at the guitar and then up at him. He leaned in and was about to whisper something but a thought flashed in my head.

I wanted him for some reason. My subconscious said I wanted him to be closer to me but the conscious me, told myself no, he is strictly just a friend.

Seth was only inches away from me and then we both closed our eyes. My brain registered what was going to happen next but I argued and fought against it.

I pushed him away again for the second time tonight.

"I think you should go home now, it's almost 11:00." I said not looking at him as he got up.

When he was about to exit the door he turned around and caught my gaze.

"Goodnight, love." He said exiting the room.

He always said that to me, every single night. But I wondered... did he actually mean it?

Chapter 2

Leaving

When I admitted to Seth how much of a loser I was the night before, we both wiped that memory out and got back to business.

Seth told me the truth about CrossStar; again my sister was right, CrossStar was supposed to be a dump. But it was supposed to be a home for more faeries than NorthStar. Seth explained how CrossStar was now his home but didn't say a word of how that came to be.

He and I started having a twisted relationship, faerie and human. I mean we always were friends and all, but I started to realize that he was a creature from another world. That helped me also back up my story to myself that we couldn't be together.

I told him about Elizabeth and her twisted fantasy. He told me about the Queen, who not surprisingly was more of a threat than her king.

Seth was staying with me at my apartment; he said it was because when you leave the realm of Fey, you can't return until everyone around you is ready. We were not to go to CrossStar until everyone around, was ready for me to leave. It might sound a little confusing but, let me tell you, it is way easier than Bio-chem.

The deal was I had to say goodbye to everyone I knew so if the worst thing possible happened, people would understand why or at least think they understood why they would never see me again.

Antoinette was the greatest of my friends, she and Seth of course.

She was tall and skinny; she hovered over me like a willow tree. She had dinner plate sized blue eyes and dark brown hair that swayed all the way down to her knees. She had one tattoo on her left shoulder; it was of a heart made out of vines which were intertwined. I was there when she got it. She said she wanted one that explained her life, so kind of like a puzzle if she was ever murdered or something like that. But after she got the tat, she promised me she would never get another, ever.

She was smart, but had no street smarts what-so-ever. But knowledge wasn't her calling in life, it was singing. Antoinette made me cry every time she talked about her singing career because she was stuck on it, but most importantly, she couldn't sing. I knew one day she would tryout for American or Canadian Idol and not even get past the tryouts, her life would end there. And now I had to leave her.

I rang the doorbell to her miniature dorm, and waited on her porch in the rain.

"Come in." her squeaky voice beckoned me. I entered nervously, trying hard to breathe evenly.

"Oh, Ely, it's you." she looked confused to see me at her house, which didn't make any sense at all, but what does now-a-days?

"Ant, I've got to tell you something." But before I could say any more my legs swayed with fatigue and my legs buckled to the ground.

"Elyon!" Antoinette gracefully picked me up into her bony but strong arms, and led me to her couch.

"What's wrong?" she began in a serious voice.

"Well, here goes nothing." I sighed. I was ready to tell Ant my story I had practiced. I made sure that each time it would be the same one so that no one would be confused or get suspicious. I wish people cared that much about me that they didn't want me to be confused.

"I still don't understand," Antoinette said holding her cup of green tea while I sipped away. "You're moving to Venice?" it seemed so hard for her to understand.

"Yes, Ant. I've been accepted at their University."

"But you're not even finished high school! How can you get into a University without any final marks?"

"I'm going to finish high school there; I even have a scholarship and everything!"

"It's just," she looked at me. Her large blue eyes didn't match her thin bony body and made her look awkward, especially with the look she was giving me now.

"I can't live without you, Ely. I never have been able to. How am I supposed to make it out there, in the world we were about to explore, if I can't make it here, in our little town of Weston?"

I looked down, trying to hide my face. I was lying to my best friend, well if she knew the truth I guess it would have been worse. She wouldn't have believed me and then they would have come, the Fey, and taken her. I could not let that happen.

Antoinette looked average when I looked up at her but then tears flowed down her cheeks and it seemed that the rain outside had transferred to her eyes. We sat there, arm in arm for a very long time then I left without any further discussion.

As I walked on, the occasional tear would slip down my cheek but when I reached the ravine the rain seemed to come out of *my* eyes. I stood there hands covering my eyes but then in between the cracks of my fingers I saw Charlie, Leslie and Mandy turning the corner. I un-clutched my face and saw Mandy waving frantically towards me.

"Slugger! Over here!" Just as an instinct I ran as fast as I could not even paying attention to where I was going or what I was doing. I knew they were never let go of this but I had to get away. They couldn't see me falling apart.

I wondered why I had gone by the La Voie River. You had to take stairs to get from the town to it so it didn't make sense why I would come here when my house was in the opposite direction.

I ran through the bush of the forest, through Cruickshank Park, down the pathway I had walked down my whole life and jumped into the wet sand box. I fell immediately with a hard impact but got up quickly and kept on racing towards the playground, the playground where I had last seen Elizabeth.

I went through the top of the play structure and curled up into a ball. I stayed like that, in the pouring rain, crying and cold.

"Liz, how could you do this to me?" I asked to no one in particular.

I stayed like that for probably an hour but then I knew that if I stayed any longer, Seth would look for me. I was trying to get up but slipped on the puddle of water under me and I slid down the slide.

I fell into the sand face first and got a heaping mass of it in my mouth. I quickly spat out the disgusting taste and cleaned myself off. Then something caught my eye.

A tall figure with blue skin and white hair stood in the middle of my towns' main river. I stared at the frightening figure long enough to realize who it was, by then it was smiling.

"Elyon" said the Queen of NorthStar. Her voice came out of her mouth like snow flakes at the beginning but ended like cold, hard hail. "Elyon, please come with me." Her voice was again soft but something about it made the hair on my arms rise.

"I'm banished from NorthStar. Remember?!" I yelled across the river so quickly I had to repeat it in my mind to understand the full potential consequences.

"Oh, no you're not." The Queens voice scratched along the water and into my ears. Already, her tone was changing. "Elyon, the King didn't mean that, he was only scared of you."

"Scared of *me*?" I asked completely confused. I shouldn't have asked that question, she wanted me to.

"Yes, dear. He is very frightened of your *potential*." I felt the moisture of the river water along my face and realized I was standing by the rivers edge.

The queen held out her hand two inches away from mine since her arms were so long.

"Come with me, Elyon. And together we could make both your world and my world at peace." Her tone was now icy and made me suspect her betrayal.

I slowly inched my hand to hers, too frightened to think, too frightened to speak, too frightened to realize this was all a trap.

My hand was almost in hers when a blue blast hit the Queen in her chest and she fell into the La Voie River. She sunk deep into the water, through the rocks, through the sand on the bottom of the river.

"Elyon!" cried a familiar voice. But when I was about to turn to see who it was, a cold icy arm reached up out of the river, and grabbed my ankle.

An icy bolt ran through my body and I cringed, almost falling into the river myself.

"Elyon! No!" screamed the same voice. Then I figured out who was calling me but now my vision was blurring and soon everything went dark.

Chapter 3

Perplexity

I woke up on the other side of the La Voie River, which didn't make any sense. The last thing I remembered was Seth, calling my name, then nothing.

I woke up cold for some weird reason, though the sun blazed down. I got up and noticed I was sitting on a pile of leaves, almost like a bed. I didn't remember making the bed, but that was the least of my worries.

The rain that poured down yesterday had made the river higher and overflow along the sides, making it larger than normal. The rain also made the river rush, so there was no chance of surviving a swim across it. So I was stuck here. The worst thing was that there was no civilization on this side of the La Voie River. The only things on this side were a few metres of sand that lead to a cliff. On top of the cliff was a forest of trees which no one had ever dared to pass.

And so I found myself stranded, only a few blocks from home.

I looked around trying to figure out a way across the rapid river. I could walk a few kilometres upstream but I was too tired and hungry to take the long hike. I could call the police, but what would I say? Hey maybe that was the best idea. I reached into my jean pocket for my cell phone.

Of course, no phone. I was hopeless. I started to laugh. I had watched this on television and in movies but I had never thought I would get to the point in which I could say 'at least nothing else can go wrong'.

After I hollered the words into the sky, and after I scared away a few birds, I was wondering if an anvil was going to fall from the sky and crash on me.

I was really at a loss. After all those years in Girl Scouts you'd think that I'd be out of this mess already. But sadly, I couldn't think of anything. All I could do was wait, until the water was safe to cross.

I sat back down and looked across the park. There were a few kids playing on the jungle gym and a few swinging on the swing set. I remembered Elizabeth and I playing like them. We'd have so much fun, but then she'd always end up talking about NorthStar. Once she started talking like that I would leave her alone. I hated listening to her stories about Faeries and creatures of the unknown, especially about the Queen. She talked about her as if the Queen was her mother or best friend. That would piss me off.

I tried to get the memory out of my head, so I turned to the Un-named Forest. Staring at it as if I were studying it, I got up again and walked closer.

I kept staring at it until something blue streaked across the trees. It was moving so fast it was just a blur, but I could tell where it had come from and in which direction it was going.

The adventurous redhead inside of me told me to adventure into the beyond, but the cautious "jetty" told me to wait. But somehow the blue streak seemed familiar, and I needed to figure out why. So I took the redheads advice.

I tried to dig my foot into the hill to lift myself up but the dirt was hard and compacted. So I took a few steps backward and got a running start at it. I got my hands firmly on the top of the cliff after I jumped. Pulling myself up was hard, but I got up…eventually.

The forest was dark green and had a full variety of trees, none that I could name. Some were strange with black heart-shaped leaves and some had black bark. It wasn't like any other forest I had ever seen.

I walked in the direction in which I had last seen the blue streak, which was away from the river. As I walked I noticed it was getting colder and colder. I tried to remember how to start a fire but failed to do so. It had been years since I had been in Scouts, now I regret missing many sessions.

I kept walking until another blue streak flashed in my vision. This time it was clearer. The colour was a dark, silky blue. The streak flitted as though it was a person, and as it flashed in front of me, a yellow silk whipped across my face. I wouldn't really describe it as yellow though; it was lighter and a bit beige. It didn't attack me in full blast; it pressed against my face in thick strands, almost like hair.

"Is anybody there?" I called into the forest but there was no answer. "Hello?" I called again. "Bonjour?

Aloha? Hola?" Well if there was a person they didn't speak English, French, Hawaiian, or Spanish. That narrowed it down.

I decided to forget about calling the creature. It could show itself when it wanted to, and so I kept on walking in the now freezing cold forest.

After a while of freezing, I took a step and noticed that there was no more forest. I was out of it. But that was the least strange thing, I turned to see the place where I had come from but the forest was completely gone. Now I only stood on dirt.

The barren wasteland seemed to go on for miles on end. I looked into the horizon and noticed the sun was setting, scratch that, the *three* suns were setting.

I sat down, wondering what to do. I was lost in a strange place, and technically couldn't get back to where I came from.

I started to cry. This was the second time in two days. I felt hopeless after crying and didn't feel any better afterwards, in fact, I felt like crying all over again but I knew that wouldn't do anything to help me find my way home.

I decided to walk towards the suns, maybe it would lead me to a payphone, I didn't know.

As I walked on, I could tell a difference in the consistency of the ground. I couldn't tell why though, because it was now very dark and the only thing that produced light were the six moons in the sky. I walked now toward these moons still with high hopes.

As I was taking a step, I plummeted through the ground or actually it seemed to be a pond. This water did not help the lowering temperature. I tried to swim to the end of the pond but my feet were bound into the soft mouldy sand that lay on the bottom. I pulled and pulled finally releasing one foot. But that didn't help so much. I couldn't pull my foot out by pushing my free foot on the sand and pulling my other because that would just lead to a never ending cycle, my free foot would get caught, get freed, get caught, get freed… etc.

I dove under the thick water and pulled my foot out with my arms and quickly swam to the surface, treading water so my feet wouldn't get stuck.

I scanned the pond using my hands, trying to find an edge and found a Cat's Tail to grab onto. I followed it to an inclining edge and used the rest of my strength to pull myself up and out.

"This is too much action for me." I said in a rough voice, realizing that was the first time I had spoken since my search for the blue streak began which was probably a day ago by now.

I sat down on the dirt; I knew this because mud started to form under me. I was breathing heavily and my body was limp. I decided to just rest there, stay there until the sun…suns came out.

I woke up in a pile of mud, made of pond water, dirt and sweat, SWEAT!? I got up, the ground was steaming hot and my hair was plastered to my face. How could the temperature have risen so quickly and dramatically? The suns blazed down on me and what used to be the mud pile was now dry dirt.

A few mirages appeared along my pathway north, and a few times I collapsed because of the major heat.

The walk across the vast land seemed to be longer than anything that I had endured throughout this crazy time period. Slowly, I made my way across the queer landscape.

After a few hours or so my stomach growled at me like a hungry bear and no matter what I did, my stupid stomach growled on. It would not shut up!

I walked and was caught by a few mirages but only one looked very real. It was a town, quaint with cobblestone streets and wooden houses. I walked to it, knowing full well that it was probably just a mirage.

A few minutes later I entered the center of the mirage stunned by its secret beauty but horrid stench. No one filled the streets and there were no signs of life. I was thinking of turning back when something grabbed my arm and pulled, dragging me to the ground.

"HELP!!" I screamed but a hand covered my mouth leaving a red halo around my lips.

"Queen better hush up, bad things happen when unknown visitors - I mean unknown *humans* enter from the CrossStar Desert." The voice was a woman's voice but what struck me the most was the fact that she called me a *queen*, the second thing that struck me was that she called me a 'human' and that meant, she wasn't.

Chapter 4

Unsatisfactory

I woke up in a bathtub, filled with dirty bubbles and a woman hovering over me.

"Ah, you're finally awake? Good, because you must be starving, while you were out like a light your stomach was having a festival."

The woman laughed and birds chirped and fish sang! Her voice was the breeze above flower fields and over the coldest mountains; a warm Chinook. I was stunned by this, her words were regular but her laughter was musical. The only reply I could handle was a small and tiny, "wow."

This time she only chuckled but still her small sounds took my breath away.

There was an awkward silence and under my breath I whispered "somebody just died".

"What was that, love?" asked the woman, I ignored what she called me and shrugged.

"I'm sorry. It's kind of like a joke me and my friend

Charlie made up. You see, in class we would always be talking and that's because every time there is an awkward silence somebody dies. That gives us an excuse to talk in class, because we don't want people dying."

"Well, it's not a very funny joke, deary, is it? But just talking isn't going to stop the dead; every one dies in the end, whether it's now or later."

I looked down into the dirty bubbles, I never thought of our little joke that way, before.

"Now, now, stop being a dragger. My name is Ma Beat, nothing else; it's already been shortened and added on."

"Elyon, that's my name don't wear it out."

"Oh I already knew that." She snickered at my little remark, and smiled. It seemed to be a remark she would say or at least an updated version of what she *had* said.

"I like you. You seem to be able to take anything, you're tough, love." She kept on washing me then pulled the plug. She wrapped me in a small towel and started to blow dry my hair with a weird machine.

"When I was about your age, my sister and I would always come to this barber, he would clean our face and do our hair, but I could never afford to keep doing it later in life…Love, may I tell you something?"

I looked at her; she had brown hair, which looked like a design which you would find on a tree or on wooden flooring. Her eyes were Granny Smith apple green and she had wrinkles around her mouth and eyes, even though she didn't look a day over 30. "Sure…I suppose"

"Well, don't fall for Beatrix's tricks, they're not worth losing you…I mean if anything ever happened to you..." She trailed off her sentences, leaving my head filled with questions.

"Why do you care so much about me?" I asked as she put away the hair dryer in a cupboard. She looked away as though she hadn't heard the question but she still answered very quietly.

"I don't want you to end up like me or Elizabeth." And at that she walked away.

Ma Beat seemed to be someone I could get along with, which had been rare enough in Weston, but in a different world... it all seemed so impossible. She understood what I'd mean without any further explanation, comments, questions or concerns. She seemed to be an older sister...or the sister of mine who had disappeared. Something strange about her also frightened me at the same time, not the fact that she had wings growing out of her back, but a dark overcast which would not let the sun in.

Everything about her was a mystery and somehow, I tied into that mystery along with my sister. Like a secret, a secret which I was not supposed to know but my sister told me when I was a child. All those secrets my sister told me, the secrets of Elizabeth.

Even though there were these secrets there were some that I didn't know.

As I sat, restlessly, at the dinner table, my mind pondered what I needed to know, not what I wanted to know.

I coughed as though to get Ma Beats attention. She looked up from her side of the round hawthorn table.

"Is there something on your mind, love?" She

was so kind, to jeopardise this queer relationship was a horrid thing to do. But I needed answers and the sooner I received them, the sooner my thirst would be quenched.

"What does Seth have to do with Elizabeth, or the Queen of NorthStar?" I closed my eyes while waiting for something; I wasn't exactly sure what, though. Maybe a beating? Or a chuckle? But after a long silence, I looked up and met her gaze.

"So you've already met Seth, huh?" I wasn't an idiot; she turned the conversation back to me, a smart move if I was a dunce.

"Yes, I met him like years ago, but he's not good at answering questions." I answered her question without any hesitation but in the process gave her the microphone and spotlight.

"Ooh, you're good, girl. I give you more respect," Finally, she acknowledged that *I* had already won this conversation.

"Lovely Seth, eh? Hmm... a very different faerie he is...very devoted...very deceitful...also full of wisdom... a bit of solitary fey though. Love, I must tell you this, those few comments are etched in stone now, and there's no more room on the rock, do you understand?"

I gave a brief nod and she seemed to relax a bit. She took an overextended sip of her rowan tea and began her lecture.

"I have never given any fey or human that many compliments, Seth is a good kid but don't over estimate his kindness or fidelity. Seth is known to all fey for his momentary unfaithfulness and solitude. But don't get me wrong; to heighten your hopes, we shall be seeing him next week." And with that she left the table.

Chapter 5

Bewilderment

I woke up with aches all over me, in my legs, shoulders and neck. The pain was almost so horrific it was unbelievable. I had a guess it was because of the long journey I had had the week before. Ma Beat gave me some ointment but it only made me smell like fish. Sometimes I didn't feel the pain because I was thinking of later today when I would see Seth again.

I acted normal throughout the morning but I couldn't stop the hope at the thought of seeing Seth. It had been or at least felt like weeks since I had last seen or heard from him and my heart was starting to tangle up again. Ma Beat finally discovered this uncalled-for edginess as I made my way to her mail box.

I took out the key she gave to me and twisted it through the lock. I could feel her eyes burning in my back and couldn't stand it any longer.

"What?" I asked turning and facing her, directly in her eyes.

"Pardon me, love?" she asked, *seeming* just as confused as I.

"Why do I feel like you're stabbing me with your eyes just then? Why do I feel like there's a grease covered mountain I'm trying to reach? Why do I feel like you're going to make me feel embarrassed anytime now?" I stared at her, she wore a confused mask but I could see through it. She knew what I was talking about. She looked confused for about five more seconds and then let out a deep heavy sigh.

"Oy love, I can't keep anything from you, can I?" She smiled and I sighed with the relief that maybe she will accept me. "It's just that, you look…I don't know… too hopeful-"

"You already know why. Seth is like my guardian angel and I haven't seen him for the past…I don't even know… how about, a very long time!"

"Yes love, I already knew that. But what I was going to say was you look like… like you're in love." I took a deep breath trying to calm myself before I said anything else.

I didn't love Seth. I couldn't love Seth and he couldn't love me. It was impossible for us to be together but I wondered has that ever stopped anyone else before?

"Told you I felt embarrassment coming." I said as my legs faltered sending me to the ground. Ma Beat ran to me but I just beckoned her to join me on the ground since I wasn't getting up anytime soon.

"But, queenie, do you love him?"

"Maybe, I don't know. He's always been there for me, I guess it's his job sort of… or it used to be." And a puzzle piece snapped itself into place.

"Seth, he left the Queen... he came here, to CrossStar...but he kept me..." all Ma Beat did was nod, and I assumed that I had to put the puzzle together myself, but, I could get somebody to check if it was correct.

"Love, don't. Right now all our focus is on peace, we don't have time for a prince and pauper relationship. Right now, we are going to the market."

This market was not anything like a regular market. Sure there were stands and bargaining was the essence but the regular bargain deals were covered by a mask of inhumanity and exhausting beauty.

The street was filled with booths and stands covered in exotic patterns and fabrics. The wording on the signs was almost recognizable as Arabic or Chinese. To add beauty were the things sold at each of these tables, odd fruits spiked or covered with hair, or clothing with embedded flowers and plates of grass.

The scariness wouldn't have been so obvious to any regular Fey but I was human. The strange faces that resembled animals or the basic element were more frightening than any horror flick I'd ever seen. Some of them had a weird script written across their faces, some only had tropical coloured skin and others well, they had no faces at all.

I felt numb while walking past them all, as they watched me with disgusted and volatile expressions. I clung to Ma Beat for support as I passed through them, like a child.

"Elyon, go find two dresses, one ragged as though you-I have no money and one elegant...outstandingly beautiful. You got that, deary?" Ma Beat asked letting go of the tight grip she had around my hand.

"Two dresses: one pretty, one not-so-much. Mm hmm." She smiled and led me off.

I walked around the booths and tried on a few dresses but none that fit Ma Beat's shopping list.

As I walked on I entered a larger tent with many racks of dresses. A pin-nosed faery with a vibrant blue Mohawk sat there, bored. He looked up at me and smiled maliciously.

"May I help you with something…mortal?" I felt a shiver of unease race through my body. I turned my body so that I was angled towards him but could still run away at any moment.

"Just looking for a few dresses, is all." I tried to sound as though I knew why I was in a faerie city. I started to browse through the dresses.

As I was looking I found one dress with blue lace and embroidered sea around the hem. My mouth hung in awe of the dress and I knew immediately that I had to buy it.

"I see you have fine taste….that dress was sewn at the shore of The Pathway River…you can tell by the wave-like hem." The pin-nosed feary explained while looking from across the tent.

"These are actual water edges?" I asked even more astonished by the dress.

"Mm hmm…I personally sewed it myself…the neck line is made of the sand that lays on Rideau La Voie."

"Rideau La Voie? I thought you said Pathway River?"

"First thing, my dear, when talking to any faery you must understand the meaning of words. You just said to me that you *thought* what I said was true. You can't imagine all of the troubles which would have happened if you get caught saying that again. You should have said 'I *heard* you say Pathway River'.

"Secondly, if you were more intelligent, you would have thought of La Voie River, which people like you usually call it, which in saying that is bad grammar. But you understood me. La Voie River and Rideau La Voie is the exact same thing-you should've known the translation… The Pathway River."

I held my breath while he was lecturing me but after I let it go, I felt my legs want to crumble-I couldn't in front of a faery- that would show weakness.

"You don't know how much sense that makes." I mumbled realizing the truth. The stupid name of the river told me not to go to the river! The Pathway River! The river from mortality to eternity!

I completely felt like an idiot and at this time that "jetty" I had talked about before, overcame me and I actually thought of killing myself, not truthfully, but I would have said it out loud in front of Antoinette.

I bought the stupid dress after all, and was now searching through bins for the other not-so-beautiful dress. As I was searching a handsome Daisy Faery walked up to me, pulling my eyes away from the bin and onto his face.

"Hello, queen… I am Korlin, what brings you here to CrossStar in the middle of the human school year?" I would have argued that it was spring break but I stared at him with wide eyes. His skin was a pale pink and his bare feet were tinted green. He wore a smug look on his face which showed age and greater intelligence than I could ever imagine. He wasn't human, obviously, none of them were.

"I'm a servant of Ma Beat's, I came from NorthStar." I lied, scared out of my wits of this feary; something about him radiated danger.

"Since when does Beatrice have servants?" he asked leaning closer towards me.

"I'm in her debt." Was all I could say, because he pulled me into a grasp which I couldn't pull myself out of. He stroked my back with his cream-textured hand, sending chills up my spine. I knew what was going to happen next. Why wasn't anyone doing anything about it? Would they let this happen to a random human on Faery territory? Was this what Ma Beat warned me about when we first met?

"Step away from my girl!" I heard a yell but I couldn't see who it was yet.

"And what if I don't?" Asked Korlin, spitting out each word he said.

A blue blast flashed before my eyes and I fell to the ground. All I could see was Korlin scramble to his feet, run away and every few seconds look back again.

Before I could know it I was pulled up from the ground into a familiar embrace.

"Elyon! Oh dear, Elyon!" I was released and finally got to see who my hero had been.

"Seth?" He nodded, smiling. Oh, how I had missed that smile. "Seth!" I rejoiced and wrapped my arms around him again. Obviously he had saved me.

"Elyon, finally! You scared me so much when I saw

you on the other side of Rideau La Voie! I tried Elyon, you have to believe me! I ran after the Queen until I had threatened her so much that she cut off her own hair just to be free herself!"

The way this moment was ending up, I could have sworn I heard the audience inside of my head cry. I started wondering again if I loved Seth and was about to ask him a question but I was interrupted.

"What's going on here?" I heard Ma Beat yelling loudly. I turned to see her trying to pry herself out of the crowd which had gathered. "Elyon, all I did was tell you to buy two dresses- oh, Seth."

She looked at Seth and nodded. I thought their reunion would have been a little different, but this worked.

"Ma Beat," Seth said, giving a polite gesture.

"My goodness, young woman, what have you done?" Ma Beat turned to me and gave me a horrified look. "Thank god that Seth was here, never flirt with Daisy Fey, they're nothing but trouble."

"I wasn't flirting with anyone! He was the one that tried to harass me!"

"She's fine and that's all that really matters" Seth cut in, he passed me a quick glare and then continued. "Ma Beat I was here in time, if I wasn't, Korlin probably would have kept her alive-but barely- at least she would have been well enough to attend the meeting tonight."

"Yes, we shall see you there." Ma Beat said, she pulled my arm and we walked away. "You haven't even bought the other dress yet!" she exclaimed. "What am I to do with you, love?"

Chapter 6

The Reason

MA BEAT AND I FOUND a ragged dress, finally. She dressed me and did my hair in a long ponytail. She didn't allow me to put on any makeup to make sure I didn't look very beautiful. That didn't help my ongoing thoughts about my meeting with Seth again tonight, either. But Ma Beat managed to pull me out of the door and onto the street.

"It's just down this road." She said, leading me into the abyss. I swore that if I put my hand up in front of me, I wouldn't be able to see it in this night.

"This is getting me nowhere, how can we possibly not be lost- or they might have given us the wrong directions." I said, gesturing to the complete darkness which surrounded us, even the sad six moons were out of sight.

"Poppycock! It's in an old tavern; it's where all of the old council members go to attend meetings, lectures or discussions."

I was about to comment on the whole 'lecture' thing but decided not to because I could see a small light-filled window coming out from the darkness.

Ma Beat knocked on the wooden door to the tavern and suddenly a very tall man opened the door in a quick swish.

"Beatrice!" He cried.

"James!" Ma Beat replied. The man who was known as James patted her on the back in a friendly gesture.

"It's so nice to see you again," He exclaimed while leading her inside. I followed slowly scanning the room for any sign of Seth

"Just to tell you though, Beat, Lance is being awfully brutal about this whole issue about the girls, you best be ready to show him who's the-"

"That's quite enough, James." Ma Beat interrupted kindly, but I noticed her little glance towards me. I glared back at her but across the room of the small pub, Seth leaned against the logged wall.

"Seth!" I exclaimed rushing towards him. I was so fast running across the room, he didn't seem to react to my embrace immediately.

"Whoa, Elyon!" He exclaimed, but he wrapped his arms around me and played with my ponytail. He leaned towards my ear so that I could feel his breath.

He began to whisper. "Elyon, you do know that this little embrace looks like something else to the elders-"

"Yes it does," said James as he passed by us.

"Oh, umm..." I let go of Seth and blushed. But all he did was smile.

"I need to talk to you about something after the meeting but right now Lance is about to kick my-" but Seth grabbed my arm and walked me to a rectangular wooden table. He and I leaned against the wall and waited for everyone else to fill the chairs.

A man with black hair, the same style as Seth's, stood up from his seat at the front of the table. He cleared his throat and then began in a loud voice.

"Welcome all elders, ex-council members-" Seth then cleared his throat loudly and passed a glance at the man. He looked at Seth and sighed. "And guest." He said looking at me.

Seth squeezed my waist. He caught my gaze and smiled. I looked at him and noticed I had to look *up* at him; last time I checked we were the same height. How long had I been in CrossStar for?

"Anyways," The man went on. "Let's get right to business, shall we? Now that the sister's heiress has entered our presence, no thanks to Mr. Ledger," He shot a harsh look across the table to Seth. "We can start making arrangement for conquering the castle. Any ideas?"

Many small discussions went on; they began as quiet little whispers until they raised their voices into yells and arguments. Ma Beat pounded her fist on the table and glared around at everyone.

Seth slowly raised his hand. Ma Beat looked at him and her evil gaze softened and her muscles relaxed. "Lance, may Seth speak?" Ma Beat turned to the man- so this was Lance- and he nodded.

"I was thinking that, since they were twins, we could pretend Elyon here was Elizabeth. We could bring her to the castle, she could explain how she lost her memory- the memory that made Elizabeth leave in the first place- and knowing the Queen, she will fall for this."

Everyone was silent for a minute then Seth continued. "Personally, I think 'no thanks to Mr. Ledger' has a pretty good idea."

I gave a giggle and stopped immediately after Lance glared at me.

"Who volunteers to take this heiress to the heart of NorthStar?" He called in a loud voice. I felt a little hurt when nobody said anything. But then Seth started laughing randomly out loud and I started wondering if he was feeling all right.

"Oh, I thought that was a joke!" Seth took a deep breath and continued. "Obviously I am."

"Also am I." said Ma Beat, she gave me a wink and I smiled.

"I know Melanie will." James called from the back. I wondered who Melanie was since I doubted she was in our presence.

"Alright then," said Lance. "You shall leave at midnight, we have a horse, Night, in the back."

Chapter 7

Left Alone

"We won't be able to pull this off," I said as Ma Beat harshly brushed my hair. I fiddled around with my dress; the beautiful one I had bought at the market. It glowed in the darkness and I was again mesmerized by it.

"I dyed my hair 5 million times; it will never be that blonde again." I was starting to doubt this whole plan, I couldn't act like Elizabeth - I barely even knew her - I wouldn't be able to lie and say I was my long lost sister.

"Where there's a will, there's a way." She said smirking. I only rolled my eyes.

"If I wanted corny lines, I would have called my mother." I said impolitely, crossing my arms in front of my chest.

"Fine then love, where there are faeries, there is always a spell to get you out of a mess." Ma Beat resolved. I heard her spit into her hands, and then they grabbed at my scalp and ran through my locks.

"EW! What are you doing?" I exclaimed, jumping up in horror.

"Working some faery magic." She said turning me to look at her.

"Faeries have magic?" I asked. I knew it was a no-brainer but I thought the whole 'magic' thing was just a... well, a fairy tale.

"Didn't Elizabeth explain what the meaning of life was to you, love?" she asked sarcastically. "I heard she told you everything, one of the reasons why she left your mother. Your mother knew she was right,"

Ma Beat took a breath and sat down on the random chair I had been sitting on. Do you want to know why it was random? Because we were in the middle of a forest, in the middle of the night!

"She knew about the Queen of NorthStar and of me," Ma Beat continued. "Your mother didn't want Elizabeth to tell you all of this. It was bad enough your sister was involved, she didn't want you getting hurt either. So one day, you might recall it, your sister told you about Seth and how he was like your guardian angel. Well, that day she told you, your mother had a fit on Elizabeth- and what should an eight year old do? She ran away- to her other mother, the Queen."

I took a deep breath and looked at Ma Beat. "So, my mother did care about me?" I asked.

Ma Beat flung herself to me and started crying and in between her tears she whispered in my ear. "Mothers always love their daughters, no matter what. Sisters love their sisters, no matter what." We stood in silence for a little bit and then Ma Beat released the embrace but kept her hands on my shoulder.

"The spell worked." She said as she grabbed a mirror off of the ground.

"What the-" I looked at my hair, which wasn't really my hair. Or was it? I stared at the bleached golden locks that dangled in loose curls. I remembered being up late at night trying to re-dye my hair that blonde. I was about to take another gasp but someone beat me to it.

I turned around to see Seth wide-eyed with his mouth hung open. I couldn't help but blush a little. I felt Ma Beats hand slip away from mine slowly so I turned around but no one stood there. It was just me and Seth.

"You look-" he began.

"Different?" I asked, taking one step towards him.

"I was going to say even more beautiful than you already are." He said, still in awe. My cheeks flared and I could have sworn I was on fire.

Seth took one large stride and ended up right in front of me. He put his hands around my waist.

"I missed you so much, never run off like that again, do you understand? Elyon I know I'm supposed to protect you from anything and everything but sometimes everything is a pretty hard job."

"Sorry, I just was really sad; I don't think I'm getting any better." Seth sank into his shoulders and I bit my lip.

"I mean," I continued. "I'm so happy you're with me, you don't know how much I love you." I swore when I realized what I had said.

I couldn't breathe. I started questioning myself

again if I was in love with Seth. What if Seth had heard me, which he probably did?

"Umm…you wanted to tell me something?" I asked changing the subject, quickly. He pulled me closer towards him so that we were only a little distance apart. He bit his lip and stared at the ground but quickly looked back at me.

"Elyon I have always loved you. Even when I was a little kid. You might love me but… but we can't be together.

"In your world, sure two teenagers together doesn't look like anything odd, but here…it's a little different." He took a breath and stared at me, "I sure don't look like it but I'm bad, I have been a spy, worked for the NorthStar guard and I have been deceitful to many fey-"

"I don't believe that," I said not completely sure what mood I was in. "I don't believe that you're evil."

"But, I am Elyon." He said leaning in closer towards me. "If faeries saw me with you I would be *hung*, they'd think I was trying to kill the heir to the throne- our saviour- even Lance thought that just now and I don't know how many oaths I have sworn to Ma Beat. We can't be together, Elyon."

I started to cry. I needed Seth, he was my guardian angel and… and…I loved him. I literally fell to the ground and cried.

Seth sat down beside me until I was finished my hysteria then picked me up as though I was as light as a feather, and held me in his arms against his chest. He kept on murmuring 'later, later, later,' but that didn't help. When we both were quiet he stood me up beside him.

"I love you, and I always will." He said through a raspy voice.

"I love you…" I said trying to hold in my new tears which were coming. I looked at him straight in the eye. I could see the hair on his arms raise as he leaned towards me and pressed his lips against mine.

I didn't react because I was just so stunned. I now knew Seth loved me but I wouldn't have expected this. It didn't seem real, the only person who I ever truly loved, loved me back- and now they had to leave. I guess the saying 'be careful what you wish for' came true. I always doubted love and said we could never be together. Now when I actually loved him, we have to leave each other.

And then I thought, well why don't I love him now instead of never loving him.

I loved Seth and everything about him was perfect compared to me. He might say that he is a traitor but I will never believe him.

Being with Seth was all I ever wanted.

He stepped back and looked at me in my eyes. "You can do this; I will always be with you. I will be with you every second, Elyon and remember I love you." Seth then slipped away into the forest.

I felt a warm hand on my shoulder and turned around; Ma Beat smiled and silently took my hand and led me to the horse.

"Night is not going to be a bother but just in case he

gets out of control just pull on the reins and he'll stop." James said as he lifted me onto Night. "You'll be fine."

Ma Beat smiled at me and stepped on a stool to whisper into my ear.

"This isn't going to be an easy journey but you have food and water this time, remember to do whatever it takes to look bad when you start seeing the city. And remember- Seth loves you and I love you too. Seth will be with you every second, just because you two love bird can't be together doesn't mean he is going to stop loving you."

And she tapped the rump of the horse and I was on my way to NorthStar.

Chapter 8

Impersonator

THE TEARS IN MY EYES had finally gone away when I reached a near by watering hole. I flung myself off of Night and onto the ground where I stood silent for a moment.

Night was a good horse, no doubt about that, but the whole ride until now had been terrible.

I'm not good at controlling my feelings, and keeping those feelings to myself is the worst thing I could do. So it doesn't help when you're riding by yourself.

All I did was think about Seth and this terrible mess I had gotten myself into. All I wanted to do was to forget and leave.

I wanted to go back home to stuffy Weston and see Antoinette if she's still alive. I wanted to go back to my horrible school and fail a few more grades before the year ends. I wanted to hang out with people and be alone in my little apartment. I wanted to call my mother and tell her I knew about faeries. But what I needed to do was save CrossStar and in doing so- save Seth.

I looked at Night. He had finished drinking from the little pond and moved onto eating some grass. I rolled my eyes and got up.

"Come on we've got to be getting to NorthStar." I said to the horse. It shook its head and kept on eating. "Seriously, we have to go." I said gesturing to the silent road. It gave me a look that I thought only people could give to one another. But Night got up and I immediately jumped on him so we could end up in NorthStar around the right time as planned.

As we rode on, I realized that Night wasn't a regular horse. The horse seemed to act like a person, acknowledging me and allowing me to acknowledge him. I figured this out as I was talking to him, mindlessly as if he could understand, I think I was a bit slap-happy.

"Could you believe that?" I asked as we crossed over a bridge. "He tells me he loves me, tells me we can't be together, and then kisses me, pathetic!"

Night shook his head and snapped it up. The horses black mane whipped my face with lots of force sending a few coughs up my throat.

The horse abruptly stopped and gave a whimper. I patted Night's head and smiled. "It's fine, really." I said as we rode on.

I looked at Night realizing his beauty in the darkness of the early morning. He was completely white with no spots or smudges of any other colour around his body but his black mane and tail. It clashed so much it took me a while until I stopped squinting. I had never seen a horse this majestically strange in my entire life.

"Were you Elizabeth's horse?" I asked trying not to sound as though he was owned by someone and didn't have a mind of his own. He nodded though. "No wonder, you're so much like her..." Night just trotted mindlessly for a while and then after a while I lost myself in the rising dawn.

*

The first thing I noticed when I woke up was that I was in a mud pile. I sat up and realized my arm was asleep from lying on it too long. I wondered how I had gotten off of Night because I had no recollection of the hours before.

I scanned the area and saw Night asleep a few meters away from me. I got to my feet and stroked his mane. "We better get going." I said as he slowly awoke.

We rode until we passed a sign which said NorthStar. I smiled thankfully that I had slept in a mud pile the night before remembering Ma Beats instructions.

As we entered NorthStar I scanned the area as though I wanted to remember it for some unexplainable reason. I had never actually seen the exterior of the city just the inside of the court walls.

It was unlike CrossStar that's for sure. Its streets were paved, just like in Weston but its buildings were very tall and made up of light grey bricks. It reminded me of a description I had read from a newspaper from

Edmonton, though I immediately doubted it once I saw the real thing.

People flooded the streets, and to my surprise; ignored me - a muddy girl on a strange horse - stumbling her way through their city. They looked like regular human beings these creatures and not like faeries at all. The men wore business suits and the women wore blouses with skirts. But there were no children in sight; I couldn't even spot kids my age.

Night walked silently through the city until we reached an enormous castle which practically glowed in its superiority. The castle reminded me of an ice version of the Emerald City in The Wizard of Oz.

We walked forward but we were suddenly halted by guards. They were all dressed in black. They were the same guards from my hearing the first time I was ever in NorthStar.

"Who are you and what is your business in NorthStar, traveller?" One of the guards yelled at me, I flinched.

"I d-don't actually know…um…my name is Elizabeth…" I lied; it hurt so much to tell them that I was my sister it made hands sweat and the hairs on the back of my neck to stand on end.

"Leave if you have no business to see the Queen." Another hollered at me. And then I had an idea.

"No, no. I must see Queen I must see her. Tell her Elizabeth's here, she'll come, I swear!" I said trying to get myself into the castle.

The guards consulted with one another for only a few seconds before they took the reins of my horse and led me inside.

Once we were through the massive doorway, they pulled me off of the horse and tied a rope around my wrists and pulled me like they were just doing to Night.

They pulled me through a long hallway with translucent walls and flooring. I was so amazed by the castle I didn't realize when I was standing still in a very large 'crystal ballroom'. Sitting in front of me in a chair on top of thousands of steps sat the Queen.

She seemed to look more stressed than last time I saw her. She gave me a glare and then seemed to look past me.

"Darren, who is this peasant traveller and what does she want with me?" the Queen looked towards a guard who was probably my height and looked about my age. His hair stood on end and was sleek black like Seth's.

"Well, your majesty, we don't actually know but–"

"You let a peasant come into my castle without any reason? How dare you!"

"She says she's Elizabeth," Darren yelled but then after a silence, he bowed down. "Your majesty."

"Impossible! Why did she come back?" She looked down at me.

"Hello, I'm right here, if you want answers why don't you ask me?" she stared at me in shock. "Queen," I curtsied. I had to remember I was trying to be like Elizabeth. The girl who was talking there was me *not* at all like Elizabeth.

"Then speak child," the Queen gestured forgiving my dispute.

I shivered and let a long gulp through my throat.

"I come from afar, your majesty. I lost my memory so it seems last night while falling off my horse, Night. I don't exactly remember where I was going but then I remembered you, Queen, and I decided to come back here. My memories are slowly coming back but I still don't understand why it was you in my mind - all I remember is that I know you, do you remember me?" I looked at her, she seemed shocked.

She flew down the stairs so fast she looked like a streak of white lightning. In a second she was in front of me staring me down.

"Elizabeth?" she asked me her face softening.

"Queen!" I yelled and wrapped my small arms around her. Her muscles tensed for a moment but then she wrapped her lanky arms around me.

"Oh, how I missed you Elizabeth," She said smiling. She pulled freely away from me and tilted her head to the side. "Now, let's get you cleaned up alright?"

A guard untied the rope around my wrist and walked me down the hall. The guard, who was named Darren, gave me a small smile and slightly waved his hand. I gave him a confused look which seemed to hurt him.

"She says she lost her memory," I heard the Queen say to Darren as I passed through the grand ballroom doors. "She needs some time to remember you, and sorry to say this but when she does... lets just say she's older now, she might not want a guard as a-"

"We'll see your majesty." And that was the last that I heard of their conversation.

Chapter 9

Blood United

When I woke, I was immediately sad and banged my head with a pillow.

"Go back to sleep! Go back to sleep!" I yelled at myself. But I got up anyway.

I expected to see a mirror looking back at me, a flowery bed side table and light blue walls. I expected to wake up in *my* room. This was not my room.

I sort of jumped as I examined my whereabouts. I was sitting on what seemed to be gold Egyptian cotton, with fabric hanging from the canopy.

The walls were painted a light canary yellow and trimmed with white. There was a fireplace across from the bed, a white couch and wood coffee table also in the room, along with a very large window draped with the same gold thin fabric which hung over top of me.

"Where are you Elyon…?"

And then I remembered.

I was in the NorthStar castle not my small apartment.

I was in a different dimension altogether. I wasn't in Kansas anymore, Dorothy.

I went up to the window, which wasn't necessarily a window; there were two large doors which led out to a balcony. I walked onto this balcony which had two lounge chairs.

I knew why I was here, not for a very good reason, but I had to smile at this beautiful sight. It was like the happy ending type of room which made me feel that maybe mine isn't so far away.

I leaned against the edge just smiling away at the pretty sight when a rock caught me off guard.

A rock went soaring through the air and landed perfectly on one of the lounge chairs. I stared at it for a moment and then looked over the balcony to see where it came from, most importantly, who threw it.

My eyes locked on Darren. I gave him a glare but he probably couldn't tell from the height difference.

He was standing in a gardens portico which was made of a mosaic pattern of round rocks.

Darren's smile widened when he saw me and he plucked a yellow flower from the ground. He reached it out towards me and suddenly it leaped out of his hands and flew upwards towards me. And there it was, in my hands. I was mesmerized by its beauty and I gazed over the edge again.

"Thank you!" I called out but Darren wasn't there. I looked at the flower confused, but I shrugged and walked into my room again.

As I was about to take a seat on the couch a young woman walked in with a maids cart.

"Awake already? It's Saturday morning. Well I guess

you of all people would wake up bright and early." She said smiling at every word.

"Who are you?" I asked in a shaky voice. It's not every day someone just waltzes into your room with a bright happy smile on their face.

"Oh yeah, Darren told me about the memory thing; You don't know how heart broken he is because of that." she said but she paused as though she said something she wasn't supposed to.

"Oops," she said with a smile still on her face.

"I just saw him in the garden, uh I know that all faeries have a special talent of their own but what's his?" She cocked her head towards the left which was strange because everyone I know -except Antoinette– tilts their heads to the right.

She looked towards the flower I held in my hands and smiled. "Levitation. I thought you'd know that one, it's really an easy one. He doesn't think much of it, if he could he would get something like clairvoyance or invisibility-" she stopped saying anything for a moment and kept her eyes still towards the cart.

"Getting a bit off topic" she muttered to herself or to me, I couldn't tell.

"Anywho, I'm Melanie, Melanie Rose. But I'd sincerely prefer if you'd plainly call me Mel, it reminds me my place in life."

This was probably the girl James had been talking about the other night.

"Mel, do you by any chance know an Antoinette? Sorry to be off topic but it seems that I have a right to be." I said gesturing towards her.

"No, no I do not. Now here's you're clothes for today.

You can't walk around in that all day." She seemed to rush through her sentence but I didn't take it personally, why did I even ask if she knew Antoinette; Antoinette is human.

I looked at the pile of clothes she held out towards me and then down at what I was wearing.

I didn't look half bad now; I wore a gold thin dress that supplied its own air conditioning device. But you could see my underwear through it. Instantly, I felt embarrassed and turned bright red.

"Its fine," Mel chuckled. "That's what these are for, there's a screen over there where you can change behind."

I grabbed the clothes from her and started changing into a light yellow thin blouse and dark blue flouncy skirt. I started wondering if Darren had seen me in my night gown from the main level but I highly doubted it, but still I felt self conscious. But I tried to take my mind off of that subject.

"What's with all these yellows, blues, gold's and browns?" I asked; Mel almost instantly started laughing her head off.

"What?" I asked again, not understanding the joke.

"Man, I don't know if you lost your memory or if you're just blonde!" She laughed to herself. She sighed and started to explain.

"They're your favourite colours! You have to remember your favourite colours, don't you? You do remember how to breathe, yes?" she started to laugh all over again.

"Stop that!" I called over the screen.

"Stop what?"

"Mocking me!" She stopped laughing immediately and didn't say a word.

I finished changing and walked around the screen. Mel was on the balcony looking over the edge. I saw she had gotten out cleaning supplies and put them on the coffee table, but I doubted that today she would clean.

I walked to the balcony and leaned beside her; she sighed but didn't turn to meet my gaze.

"Sorry about that, I didn't mean to hurt your feelings, I know how sensitive humans are but…in the time that you were gone I kind of lost myself, too."

She looked at me now and I gave her a forgiving look. Melanie patted her back unexpectedly which made me confused.

"I'm not a faerie, Elizabeth. But I'm not a human either - well, not anymore at least. I used to live where you did, in Weston, like any other human there. One day I met this wonderful man, I was probably a few years older than you are now, and he just took my breath away. Needless to say I fell in love with him and he fell in love with me. We married 5 years after we met and a few years after that we had a little girl. But then the world took a dark turn for the worst.

"Now this mans name was James, and he decided right after we brought our little girl home to tell me he was a faerie. I believed him immediately, I don't exactly remember why but I did, I just knew in my heart that he was telling the truth. Of course that didn't compensate for my anger and rage. I told him to leave and never show his face again but he said he couldn't.

"You must know of the rule that if humans or faeries

alike are not ready for you to change you won't, am I correct?" I nodded briefly listening so closely to every word and even every emotion she was presenting me.

"Well, he told me then. He told me only both of us could leave, but the baby must stay. I was torn. James told me I had to leave since I knew. Looking back, I wish he never told me.

"But we left; we both lived in CrossStar together for the longest time. I know, I know. I lived in CrossStar but back then it was just a rural version of NorthStar, for people who didn't like the big city.

"Anyways, we lived there for probably 8 months, just settling down when the rebellions started and their interest in me grew. I was taken away by the Queen who said she should've had me-" she looked at me funny, kind of like an apology but more like she let a secret out.

"Please, tell me you don't remember why you left, please tell me I didn't just remind you." She begged for an answer. I looked at her but shook my head, it sort of felt like I couldn't speak anymore. She nodded and cleared her throat to continue her story.

"The Queen made me an Elemental, a creature formed by another taking the shape or form of an element."

"Which Elemental are you?" I asked. She seemed astonished by these words as though she wouldn't have pictured them on my lips or Elizabeth's.

"I'm a Sylph, and air elemental, which can only be woman. But Sylphs always stay young and never, and I mean never die. Sure you age a little but then you practically reincarnate into a teen again, which is why I only look a little older than you when I'm actually 45."

"You're 45!" I asked surprised by this anomaly. She nodded giving me a small smile.

"But forever I stay this way, stuck in my twenties and a maid for the rest of eternity."

"Did that sound as profound to me as it did to you?" I asked smirking.

"Oh yes it did." She said smiling. She seemed happy, and I couldn't help but feel at peace with her, it was like having my mother with me, which reminded me—

"What happened to your daughter?" I asked quietly not trying to hurt any of her feelings as possible.

"The Queen allows me to see her through a looking glass to see if she's alright. She used to live with one of my good friends until she moved out illegally and bought her own house. She's probably your age now." She bit her lip and leaned closer to me with her hand cuffed around my ear.

"You probably already know that she's fine but, I see Elyon in the looking glass, a lot of the time. She moved to Venice for a scholarship. I'm the only person in the Kingdom who knows about her and trust me it'll stay this way." I tried hard not to laugh but then something caught me off guard.

"How does Elyon find her way into your daughter's life?" Mel paused for a little bit and then looked at me straight in the eye.

"Elyon's her best friend."

Chapter 10

Recollection

After our long conversation, Melanie left. She actually did end up cleaning my room before she left but without further discussion.

I sat alone in Elizabeth's room for a while until the Queen came and escorted me to breakfast.

The breakfast room was a long hall and the table we dined at had 25 chairs, but only me, the Queen and King ate there.

The breakfast was absolutely to die for. I had an omelette with exotic fruits tucked away inside. I also enjoyed a large slab of French toast, which the Queen said was made out of a sugary type substance out of strawberry dew: not sugar.

The breakfast was wonderful but the Queen and King weren't the liveliest people I had ever met. The King barely said a word not to mention made any conversation. And all the Queen talked about was politics and war, not my forte.

I couldn't help but feel like I was missing something; the Queen seemed to watch my every move and the King seemed to watch the Queens every move.

The King didn't act like the regular rulers of society, he appeared to be uncomfortable with me around, I remember the first time I had met him, he was strong willed and looked powerful but there was no doubt that back then the Queen had more authority and dominance. Now the King acted as though he was the jester, he had no power whatsoever.

The Queen on the other hand appeared to be cautious or aware of *me*. I remember her saying that the King was scared of me but it seemed he was more scared of her and she was more scared of me which led me to think about... what scared me?

The Queen acted like my tour guide for a while, showing me around, forcing Elizabeth's memory on me. It was obvious she was trying to make me remember why I came here... or why Elizabeth had left, but honestly I didn't know.

I asked her random questions like: 'what's my favourite sport?' or 'name three things I'm good at'. But I asked her once who my real mother was and she was silent, she asked me in return: "Do you remember her, too?"

I shook my head silently; I paused and tried to think of another question to ask.

"But I do remember living with another female, in my memories everyone says she looks like me but I think she doesn't look like me at all."

"Well spoken." Was all the Queen said.

She showed me the garden which I had seen Darren in during the early hours of the morning. She also showed me the kitchen, another ballroom and many other rooms which didn't inspire me.

We kept on walking down a long hall until the Queen stopped me again.

"This is the library, would you like to enter it?" she asked me gesturing to the open door. I nodded and led myself in.

I stared at the rows and rows of books. There were so many of them you could tell that they had to make extensions on the shelves to the ceilings.

The shelves were a dark brown and the carpet was a pool table green, the only real colour was the small and different amounts of colour from the spines of each book. I sighed at the magnificent sight. The one percent of my body that followed the stereotype 'nerdy' was my love of books, and this love seemed to expand as I ventured further into this truly beautiful library.

"Would you like to stay here for a while? Catch up on some history?" asked the Queen, who I had forgotten was there.

"Yes please." I answered in a small voice. The Queen left me silently without another word and I continued my walk through the library.

Each time I saw a book I wanted to read, I would put it in my large sling back bag as I explored this never ending library.

I had probably picked up 30 or more books when I realized my bag was ripping at the seams and I decided to get reading these books.

I scrambled trying to find a book to read knowing

that some of the books the Queen wouldn't want me to take out.

I grabbed one gilded book and brushed off the dust that had formed on the cover. The books title revealed: *"Journal of the First Life of the Beats"*. I opened to the first page where there were two entries in the journal of two different italics. I decided to read the penmanship which was legible:

"August 27th, 1650 (human reference)
Today, my mother bought me and my sister this journal. We both have to share it, and I don't really care, but Beatrix minds. She wants her own and doesn't understand that it's expensive for a journal these days, well with the Separation Divide and everything- who knows maybe humans will try to expand the divide to NorthStar, which would be funny! It's a wonder why father likes her best, she isn't going to be a good ruler if that's what she wants. There I said it, if you're reading this Beatrix you read what I wrote correctly, now go and tell on me!"

I was startled by the first entry, 1650! How old is this book anyway? But also I've heard that name before somewhere, Beatrix, didn't Seth call Ma Beat something like that? No, he called her *Beatrice*, there's a difference. But the title is Journal of The First Life of the Beats, maybe Ma Beat and this Beatrix person are related, what if this was Ma Beats journal, and it sounded enough like her to be.

But also what did it mean by Separation Divide? And how 'the humans' were expanding the divide to

NorthStar? I had a feeling I didn't know my history very well after all.

I wanted to find another entry by this person who might be Ma Beat. I searched a few pages and finally found one.

"*August 30th, 1650*

Today we learned about pre-history in class. It's actually very interesting.

Humans have always had men as the primary species but in the Fey dimension it is much different. Women were the primary species.

Fate, the Queen of queens was in fact the first faery ever; even more of a shocker is that she was human. *Since she was the first faery she was given the responsibility to rule the Fey Kingdom. She always ruled alone until Fey had been divided and then other Queens came. The queens found lovers and married making Kings also in charge, kind of like the human world.*

Now the reason why we call human girls queens is because they were originally the first faery monarchs."

There's another hint how this is possibly Ma Beat; the first time I met her she called me *queen*.

I decided to try to read the next entry even though it was twice the size of the last one and I had to squint to understand the cursive writing:

"*Tuesday,*

Today Angelica bought Beatrice and I this journal, though she will barely use it…

I still complained that we should get separate ones so we

couldn't read each others ongoing thoughts that day…(if you don't mind I like a little privacy.)…

I met the Royal Guard today and this one man, human if you will, seemed to fancy me, dare I say it so do I! I never understood this history stuff and he explained it to me and it made so much more sense…

The humans and fey creatures once lived in harmony with one another which is why people very rarely are born with pure fey blood or pure human blood, it's usually half and half (like me!)…

We all lived together, there was no Faer only Earth. Then many other creatures were being developed and the dimension started forming and then finally humans and fey were the last to live together…they lived together peacefully but they knew separation was the best. Some faeries stayed on earth but most fled to an abandoned planet soon to be NorthStar.

When the humans started creating different government for different countries the faeries weren't allowed position because we still used a monarchy, which still seems to be the smartest way to solve things…

Soon I will be monarch of all NorthStar and then Aether, the Ago Planets and Faer City, who ever said absolute power corrupts absolutely was a dim wit…"

I heard footsteps coming towards me and I shoved the journal back into my bag and took out the rest.

"Shall we eat dinner now?" asked the Queen.

After dinner, which was delicious, I went back to my room and decided to get dressed for bed which I was almost dying for.

I learned from this mornings experience that I was

going to wear sweats and a tank top to bed. I searched the dressers for a while but I couldn't find any clothes that met my standard. I was just staring at the drawers when I heard someone enter my room.

I saw Mel leaning against the doorway; she was wearing a flowing dress that was solid blue. She was tossing a ball, it seemed, up in the air then catching it and repeating this pattern over and over again.

"Can't find anything to wear?" she asked walking towards me. I nodded my head and stared at the ground. I looked back up at her and noticed she was right beside me. It also wasn't a ball she was tossing but some sort of three dimensional hexagon. Melanie sighed.

"Want to play a game?" she gave me a one sided smile. I shrugged.

"Do you have any sweats?"

After a while of more searching we found a pair of soft fabric pants and a thin T-shirt, it was the closest thing that would suffice.

Mel and I sat in the garden as she explained the rules to me for the game. "It's pretty simple actually, what ever space the dice *lands* on, not the one that you *can* see, you answer the question, it's kind of like a mix of 'truth or dare' and 'would you rather'. Other than answering the questions it's an easy game."

She took the deformed dice and tossed it in the air, once it was tossed the sides glowed and writing appeared. She let it fall this time, which seemed to make time stop in the process. Once it hit the ground it froze in place without a second bounce which startled me. The spaces stopped glowing and Melanie picked up the dice. The space that the dice had landed on continued glowing.

"'Would you rather live forever but alone or live with the love of your life for a short lifespan'?" Mel read from the small space. She looked up at the sky and then at me.

"I'm already living alone for my whole life but only living with James for a little bit and then losing him I think wouldn't be the greatest choice, how about you, Liz?"

A lump in my throat immediately developed when Mel called me my sisters' nickname, I felt like an impersonator, which technically I was, but it made me feel sick to my stomach.

"I don't know, they both sound so horrible, but in a way *I'm* living with the one I love but we can't be together forever, so both options suck I guess." Mel laughed at my answer but she didn't question who I was talking about but in a silent whisper I called a cry for help. "*Seth.*"

Melanie and I played the game for probably three more hours until all the questions were being repeated. "It's not supposed to do that," Mel explained. "It changes once you read it but maybe because you're human it doesn't want to change."

I had gotten so tired that I fell asleep sometimes and Mel shook me hard to wake me up and she decided she was tired also. She insisted on carrying me to my room, which she probably could do because she was so tall, but I refused. I wanted to explore the garden a little deeper but I promised Mel I'd only be out for a little bit more.

I walked around the portico, and fell in love with the night scenery. I glided through the yellow flowers and bright green plants which were still visible in the moonlit night.

I walked under a few terraces covered in ivy and vines until I reached the center of the enormous garden. And in the center was a beautiful fountain surrounded by luscious roses.

I didn't know what took over me, I think I was finally in a place where I felt safe and I decided to dance around.

I danced as though I had a partner with one of my arm around an imaginary neck and the other in an imaginary hand. I sang a song I remembered from a Disney movie as a kid, I think it was from Sleeping Beauty... Yes! It was 'Once Upon a Dream' I remember the song now:

"I know you
I walked with you once upon a dream.
I know you
The gleam in your eyes is so familiar a gleam
Yes, I know it's true
that visions are seldom all they seem
But if I know you, I know what you'll do
You'll love me at once-"

"-The way you did once upon a dream." My heart jumped as I felt heat slip under my arm and wrap around my hand, I wasn't dancing with an imaginary person anymore. A pale face stood in front of me and continued spinning me around, though I was just frozen solid.

"So you like dancing by yourself but when you get a partner you won't dance anymore?" the person asked as they stopped dancing.

"Seth? But how-" I stared blankly at him for a moment, and I felt embarrassed for singing, but then a rush of relief went through me as I remembered I was wearing sweats this time.

"Hey, you think I never watched Sleeping Beauty?" He asked a little smug.

"No, it's not that, but why did you come here I mean-"

"You called for me, I'll always be here for you." He slipped my arm away from his neck but took my hand in his. He leaned closer towards me but I pulled my hand free and placed it on his mouth.

"Okay, I'll let you kiss me right now if you agree to my terms."

"What terms?" he mumbled through my hand.

"That you stop cutting off my every sentence." He laughed and moved my hand gently away from his face.

"You know I can't agree to that." He said smiling and he was still smiling as he kissed me.

I felt the whole world swirl around me and I felt my head getting dizzy. I felt Seth tap me on the shoulder and I noticed I was lying in his lap, the suns were peaking up over the horizon but the moons were still in the sky.

"Good morning, Elyon." He whispered as he kissed my cheek. "I have to get back to CrossStar now."

"No don't leave me again," I said holding his arm close to me. "I love you too much."

"I love you too but I have to go and I never actually left you, don't be silly. I have always been right here. If you ever need me I will be right here."

"I need you right now, don't leave me." I whispered. I was still really tired and I felt myself falling back asleep.

Chapter 11

Death Wish

I woke up in Elizabeth's room again, but there was a note right beside me. I picked it up, still half a sleep, and read it out loud:

"Elizabeth-
Please remember our last song
Please forgive what I did wrong
Please forget why you left
Please escape from our hearts regret
Please love me again
Please love me again
-Darren"

I closed my, apparently hanging, mouth shut with a snap. What was with Darren and Elizabeth? Did they have chemistry before my sister randomly disappeared? Was Darren still in love with her? Whatever the reason was I had to figure it out so I wouldn't hurt this poor guys feelings.

I got out of bed and walked to the screen which hid the journal I had found in the library. I doubted it would hold any answers but it was nice to check.

I decided to flip to a random page and start reading even if it was the girl with the nasty hand writing.

I opened the journal; the pages slid and I stared at the entry and was relieved it was the girl named Beatrice's writing on the page:

"Saturday, late at night
Drew just announced that Beatrix shall get NorthStar and I shall get a silly rural city called CrossStar, I haven't even heard of it before!

Sorry to sound like my sister but I am deeply depressed. I am moving tomorrow to this city and I have already said my goodbyes. Luckily Lance is coming with me! He proposed the other day and I am getting married once we reach CrossStar! I am very excited but shocked; I wanted NorthStar to be mine so bad! I think Drew created CrossStar just now to get me out of the city! I am crying right now just writing this stupid entry.

On the other hand the humans have split from the faery world entirely now, they don't even want good trade or cross marriages, I never liked humans, they're all pigs! They made my mother and Drew divorce in the first place. (Divorcing is some silly practice created by some Henry person monarch.)

Drew also said that I was in charge of the element fire which is absurd, he knows that I'm deathly afraid of the that magic, and Beatrix is in charge of the ice element which is *absurd because she would always cry for a blanket when the sun went down as a little fey.*

Anyway it's late and the queen is calling lights out."

I sat still, almost frozen. This *was* Ma Beats journal and supposedly her sister is the Queen. I was shocked and appalled by this.

Ma Beat was related to this nasty creature? And Elizabeth liked the Queen, who it seems shouldn't have gotten the throne.

I thought for a long time and this one entry explained almost everything I was looking for.

It perfectly stated that CrossStar wasn't a regular city and that Ma Beat is its ruler, she is hot tempered and thinks herself as high and mighty. So did Lance, the man at the meeting, which meant James was Melanie's husband also.

It also perfectly stated that the Queen, Beatrix, was cold and didn't have a kind bone in her body, she was made of ice.

I also just figured out why Elizabeth left. She had run away from the Queen, I mean Beatrix. Elizabeth had figured out that the Beatrix was evil. But my last question now was: why was she so evil?

Melanie came shortly after with my clothes and I was off to breakfast. The day seemed to fly by but there was a stiff tension in the air, Beatrix seemed to be smiling a lot and the King, who I wouldn't have been surprised if he was that guard Beatrix was talking about in her journal entry, was out of sight.

The Queen finally pulled me aside after lunch, which was more delicious than yesterdays.

"Elizabeth, have you recalled any new memories lately?" she asked playing with my hair.

"Yes actually," I bit my lip and looked down; I could feel Beatrix's hand tense as it continued stroking my bleached locks.

"Me and Darren... I remember a lot of him. And I remember my real mother... in the human realm?" I asked if I was remembering things right and she nodded, full of relief. I could have told her *'yeah I remember why I ran away from you in the first place, so if you don't mind I have a horse to catch'*, you wish.

"Darren and you were in love, I could hardly blame you, and he is a wonderful boy. So loyal and kind, any girl would kill for him. But yes you were born in the human world and raised there until you found me, I changed your life."

"But my mother - in all my memories she's angry at me, didn't she love me?" I kept my gaze to the floor not wanting to look Beatrix in the eye.

"Yes she loved you, what mother wouldn't love her child? But she didn't understand you as well as I do." She lifted my chin up and wiped away a tear that had slipped through my eyes.

"I also remember, another boy, he looked kind of like Darren, his name was Seth." I looked at her straight in the eye but she didn't immediately respond.

"Maybe he was someone from your childhood; I never had any subjects named Seth."

"Ledger was his last name." She glared at me, I

didn't think she wanted to show me it but she let it out.

"Anyway," she said introducing a subject change. "There's something I need to tell you. You see the people of NorthStar don't trust you anymore, since you left us. The only way to gain their trust is to become Queen." I stared at her blankly with my mouth hanging open.

"You have got to be joking."

"I assure you I am anything but. The only way you can become Queen, obviously, is if you wed."

"You mean if I get married!?" I asked astonished. I've seen many movies and read lots of books when kids my age or younger get married, but me? I never even thought about getting married, not even to Seth!

"Yes, and the only way that's going to happen is if you meet a suitable partner, and the only way *that's* going to happen is if I host a ball."

"You mean a dance?"

"Elizabeth, I have taught you better than to question the obvious and this is the last time I will say *yes*." My mouth still hung open and I blinked a few times to bring myself back to reality.

"The ball will be tomorrow night," she continued. "You must use dance cards to keep track of who you are dancing with, they're really just a piece of paper with the names of the people you should dance with, and it just simply hangs around your wrist by a string."

"So I have to find a husband tomorrow night?" I asked, scared if this question would break the rules.

"You actually have from 10 to midnight, not a whole lot of time but I can guess the top five already." She said smiling.

"I personally can't wait, and then you'll have a day of rest but then the next day you will wed! Isn't that perfect? Right after you wed we'll have a crowning ceremony, busy schedule but I think you'll be alright won't you?" I stared blankly at her.

"Are you trying to kill me?" I asked taking a deep breath.

"Oh, you'll be fine." she said wrapping her arm around my shoulders. "Queen Elizabeth, doesn't that sound so perfect?" I rolled my eyes, *poor Queen Elizabeth; she probably didn't have a lunatic pressuring her into these kinds of things.*

Melanie was cleaning my room and I was sitting on the edge of my bed swaying my legs all over the place. Melanie was going to help me get ready for the Ball tomorrow night though I didn't think her help would be enough.

Melanie clapped her hands. "Stop moping around and help me out. Do you have *any* idea who you would like to marry?"

"The Queen showed me a few people but none of them… pleased me?" I looked at her and she rolled her eyes. "But I was thinking about-"

"Who? Tell me who!" she said squealing, she was acting like a little girl at a sleepover; which reminded me when I was asking Seth who he liked, so I giggled. But who did he like then? Was he talking about me?

"I was thinking of… maybe…Darren."

Melanie had her mouth hung wide open. "Are you serious? The Queen will *kill* you if you ask him to be your consort."

"Seems like she's already trying." I shrugged.

"Wait this means you got your memory back!" she said almost jumping onto the coffee table.

"Well, at least most of it."

"Tell me what you remember, *all* of it!" I was kind of wondering what I missed out on in life to deserve Melanie acting like this.

"A. I remember Darren, you already know that part. B. I remember my real mother. C. I remember Seth, and don't tell me he doesn't exist." Her expression didn't change.

"Why would I lie to you?" she asked.

"Because the Queen did."

"But the Queen has things against you, Liz."

I rolled my eyes at the nickname but she probably thought it was at the statement.

"So Seth actually does exist?" I asked, just for confirming reasons

"Yes, and the two of you were good friends, not in the way like you and Darren but like BFF's as kids would say." She giggled and I wondered if she was just happy to be living like a teenager and not looking like one. "Seth was such a nice boy; he was a year older than you, though."

"Really?" I asked stunned, he never told me that!

She nodded. "You two always hung out until Darren got a job here, too. They're brothers, you know." She nodded again answering my unspoken question.

"Then you guys just weren't as attached. You fell in love with Darren and Seth kind of felt useless. But you changed that. You gave him the toughest job in the world. You even got it established by the Queen. You made him Elyon's guardian angel."

A tear dripped down my cheek and Mel, confusedly, wiped it away.

"When you left, so did Seth," Mel continues, "He is called the Betrayer for leaving the Queen and working for CrossStar but he really truly isn't. He is in fact the opposite because he didn't betray anyone; he is still looking after Elyon this very second." She stared out over the balcony and past NorthStar, through the desert and back to Weston.

I studied Melanie's face until I could take it no more.

"Melanie, there's something I have to tell you." She looked at me with a confused expression.

"The only way you'll believe me is if I technically show you."

"What do you mean?" she asked.

"Where's the looking glass?"

Melanie led me through a series of halls and rooms. We finally stopped at a massive door at the end of the left wing.

She opened the door to reveal a broom closet, I raised my eyebrow but she kept on moving through. She pressed her foot hard on a random black tile and the closet doors slammed shut.

"You need to close your eyes now, or you'll figure out how to get here again."

"Is that a bad thing?" I asked and immediately she nodded.

I closed my eyes tight and to my surprise she

trusted me enough to keep them just like that, without a blindfold or something rather.

For the rest of our journey to the looking glass it was all black for me and a series or sharp turns and tightrope walking.

"We're here." she finally said. And I opened my sore eyes.

The room was pitch black except for a shining mirror in the center of the room. We reached it in three or five steps.

"How does it work?" was my first question of a series.

"You ask it what you would like to see."

"Can you ask where any person is or do have to know the person or be related, etcetera."

"The person must know *you*. This is a looking glass. It isn't some stalker device."

"Perfect." I stroked its frame. Silver roses twisted out of metal and other metal works around it. "Ask where Elyon is or to see her, please?"

"But she doesn't know me." Melanie looked at me confused but she obeyed. "Show me Elyon Wuerch." I closed my eyes waiting for screaming or at least something but nothing happened.

I opened my eyes and looked at the looking glass; it showed me, and staring straight back at me it also showed Melanie with no expression on her face.

"It does this sometimes, I'm sorry; it's been doing this lately. I can tell that you wanted to see your sister-"

"Don't you get it?" I asked moving her head to look at the piece of reflective glass. "I'm not Elizabeth, I'm

Elyon! The looking glass *is* working!" Mel stared at me for a little bit but then her eyes widened.

"That explains so much! How you lost your memory, you didn't actually but you were trying to get information. How you didn't know things about yourself! You're Elyon! Oh my god, you're Elyon! The Queen will *kill* you if she finds out you've been lying about your sisters' identity!"

"That's why I only trust you with this secret, Mel. Wait, why would the Queen kill me? Is it because I'm *banned* from here?"

"Yes if she finds out, but she'll kill you anyway. What I mean by that is she was going to kill you, I mean Elizabeth in the first place, at the coronation. Then kill you, Elyon. Killing you right now is like killing two birds with one stone."

Chapter 12

Self Betrayal

I PLAYED WITH A DANGLING piece of hair which was not pinned up in my tight bun, which tore at me scalp.

Melanie finished preparing my dress and gave me a smile. "You're doing the right thing, and you know the plan, Stan" I took a deep breath.

"I don't think I can hurt Darren or Seth or Elizabeth like this." I sighed.

"They'll all understand, Darren will quickly gain allegiance when you marry him-" "But that's like using him! He *thinks* Elizabeth is alright when I don't even know if that's true!"

"Elyon, I know this is hard for you, but you have to do this, for the sake of everyone."

I looked away trying not to let the tears escape my eyes. It seemed ok when I was acting like sensitive Elizabeth but now I was me, and I knew Melanie would know and expect nothing but my usual reputation.

The dress I wore was a simple navy one strap

dress, but what made it beautiful were the five million flickering stars on it. Mel said they were from the east sky and this dress was a painting of them. I know the fey world could be so complicated at times.

Melanie quickly put some makeup on my face, just a simple cover-up, some version of mascara and dark red lipstick. Personally, I'd usually go for some eye shadow and cheek tint but right now she was the boss.

The Queen came quickly after and handed me the dance card which I put on my wrist. She led me to the main gate, where we were both greeted by guests of all sorts.

"Elizabeth! Oh I remember when you were just a little girl, well look at you! You're all grown up." Some lady said as she pulled me into a bear hug.

"She lost some of her memory, Spelca. I'm so sorry, when she fully remembers I'll have you over for tea one day." The Queen said quietly as Spelca entered the ballroom.

I looked down the pathway where the guests were coming from and saw eight or ten guards surrounding a small carriage. The carriage stopped right in front of us and a tall woman exited out.

She had long sleek black hair that went down to her knees in a *Cleopatra* style with the cut bangs and everything. She wore a beige Egyptian cotton dress with a gemmed collar. More guards followed behind her.

"Fate, how wonderful to see you, your majesty." Beatrix bowed; I looked confused at her but bowed anyway.

"I don't think we have met," the woman said in a

snake-like French accent. "I am Fate, Queen of Faer City."

"I'm Elizabeth; it's an honour to meet you." I replied bowing again.

"None of that child if you don't know my power or capabilities." She smiled. I nodded. "I shall talk to you later." Fate said to Beatrix.

She gave me a quick wink before entering the ballroom over her shoulder. I frowned and looked up at Beatrix, but she didn't seem to notice.

"Are you ready?" the Queen asked. I would have probably said no if she knew who I was but I wasn't planning on telling her that just yet.

My legs began to ache after an hour of standing by the door and the worst part was yet to come, the dancing part. The most recent time I had danced was with Seth in the garden. But before that, I hadn't danced since I was 6 or 7 when I quit ballet class because the teacher couldn't pronounce my last name right. She kept on calling me *Miss Wuch* and after a little while of it, great posture wasn't worth it.

As I entered the ballroom, a whiff of brown hair smacked me in the face. "Ow!" I cried.

"Sorry, Liz." A squeaky voice called. I looked at Mel, she was wearing a black dress with a white bow on the bottom left corner. She was also carrying a platter of wine glasses filled with an orangey liquid.

"Why are you here?" I asked as I followed her to a table.

"The Queen asked me to keep an eye on you while she's talking to the guests." I looked at her stunned.

"Well then, who should I dance with first?" I asked. She grabbed my dance card in a swift motion.

"I suggest dancing with the 'no's' first and then the fifth last should be Darren. So I'd go with Sir Bernard of Cale, he is definitely a no."

"Why do you say that?"

I looked down at my feet as Bernard spun me under his arm. Don't take it the wrong way, he was a great dancer but I don't want to marry someone who I have to *duck* to spin under their arm, if you know what I mean.

He kissed my hand and then almost immediately after I crossed his name off twenty times.

"Harsh, don't you think? Do you discriminate height?" Melanie said over my shoulder. I laughed.

"Have you ever seen my real life?" I thought about all the people who have hated me for good reason and even what my friends have done in the past.

"That's just a cover, you're always nice when you're around An-" I obviously knew what Mel was about to say but I didn't think much of it.

"Next." I said as I handed her the dance card

"Matthew Carmichael of Sythine." I gave her a questioning gaze.

"Are you sure?" I asked. She nodded.

"Why?"

"Because I swear I know a Matthew Carmichael from school."

"They obviously can't be related. Just go and dance with him or you'll be behind soon.

So I danced with this Matthew guy and a few others

who Mel would call *Obvious No's*. But when it was time to dance with Darren, I didn't feel calm the way I did with the others.

I slowly walked up to him. "Hey." I said giving a weak wave. He smiled, which made me happy and full of betrayal at the same time.

"I got your note." I said smiling weakly.

"You did, did you?" he asked looking above my head. He was only a little bit taller than me but enough that I couldn't lie and say *I* was taller. I began thinking about what Mel had said earlier about me discriminating height. I don't think I'm really against short people but *I* just hate being short.

"Yeah I did and... I just wanted tell you that I remember." He smiled now so brightly he reminded me of a little boy.

"Would you like to dance, Elizabeth?" He asked and I nodded and pretended to smile, he seemed so happy it hurt me so much to lie to him.

We danced a little but then the song changed to a much slower song, darn it! But he lit up and stroked my face softly.

"Do you remember this song?" he asked. I nodded slowly and he pulled me closer towards him gently. Darren compared to Seth was a feather and Seth a bulldozer but I'm not saying that Seth isn't gentle. It's just that, this was scary gentle, like handling sand and not wanting one grain to slip away.

"I missed you, you can't believe how much I did." he said as I relaxed my head on his chest.

"Darren... I love you but, I'm still not entirely sure about everything. So much has been going on the past few days and-" He pulled himself away from me and smiled.

"I completely understand." And from then on we just danced like everyone else in the room, not like how much Darren loved Elizabeth and not like how much I was betraying him.

I sat down for a little while holding back my tears, which made me *behind schedule* according to Melanie.

Finally she made me dance with the last few and then the Queen called out in a loud voice:

"People of Faery, may I have your attention please. Finally after years of absence my daughter has returned! Please give a round of applause to Elizabeth!"

Clapping surrounded the entire, massive ballroom. Melanie pinched my side and I jumped up, even more clapping arose. I sat back down almost immediately; I didn't like *this* sort of attention.

The queen cleared her throat again:

"As you all well know that today is the Proposal Ball for Elizabeth. May I have all the wonderful gentlemen wanting her hand stand up for an applause also." Again a round of applause.

"Now, will all of you please enter the waiting room?" All the men I danced with exited the Ball room and entered another. Melanie gestured for me to follow and I did.

Beatrix started to talk about something else but I didn't listen, my head was full of too many thoughts that I couldn't even sort them out.

I walked mechanically towards the room wondering how I could say no to all those men, and how I could say yes to Darren.

I entered the room quietly and closing the door behind me, I realized that this was the hallway I had been in just the other day during my tour, and the closest other room for privacy was the study which was even a little ways away. I gulped and cleared my throat to get their attention.

"I'm going in random order so don't feel like first is the worst and second is the best." They all laughed at my kiddie joke, but I saw Darren rolling his eyes which gave me a little hope for this bunch of men.

"Lewis Dughem." I called out across the crowd. A lanky man stood up, probably in his late twenties or so, one of the oldest here. I remember the Queen chose him in her Top 5 the other day but Mel put him as a No.

I walked with him to the study, he was talking about some sport that I didn't have a clue about and boasting about how good he was at it.

Once we reached the study he immediately took one of the chairs in front of the desk, not the one behind the desk where I was planning to sit, which I was honoured by that he had some respect for woman.

"Mr. Dughem-"

"Please, call me Lewis."

"Okay then, Lewis, can I just ask a few more questions before…"

"Sure." He immediately said.

"Umm…where did you grow up?"

"That's a simple question, one of the Ago Planets, Glacée; I think that's the translation into English. But I was raised on Fire, the other Ago planet."

"You mean Ice not glacée." I corrected.

"Sorry, the language on Ice is very similar to French,

it's why most Faeries speak it, or use it as a translation, like Rideau La Voie!" I nodded, but it still didn't make sense to me, if you can translate it to French, why not English?

"What was it like there?" I asked leaning forward.

"On Ice or on Fire? I don't remember much of Ice but I just remember the ice-like ground and the frostbitten sky. Now Fire was very interesting. You'd think of it as a fireball-planet, but actually it's more or less the same as here. The ground is rocky in some places but it has more greenery than Ice. The only reason they call it fire is because yes there are fire storms but it is the exact opposite of Ice. It is my favourite place in the entire universe, especially the small quadrant I grew up in."

"I prefer small towns also; I grew up across La Voie River, in Weston?"

"Yes I know the place, very quaint isn't it?"

"Yeah but it still gets its share of troubles."

"It did, did it?" he asked smirking at the obvious idea that Elizabeth did crimes, in your dreams.

"Lewis you seem like a very nice man but I need someone who can protect me no matter where or why, in another lifetime maybe." He smiled and kissed my hand.

"Thank you, for giving me the chance." He got up and walked towards the door.

"Wait! Don't tell the others that you weren't the one who I chose and could you please send Fredric of FrontGate."

"Will do, your majesty." He said and then left the room.

After a little while Fredric entered the room. He

was tall, but well built and had a gorgeous smile. I probably would have dated him in Weston if we had met under normal circumstances.

"So you're from outside of Faer City?" I interrogated.

"It's just a small town, everybody makes a big deal about it but really, *you* could live there for all I care." He said with a smirk.

"I heard that only, umm... dead fey can live in Faer City."

"Yes, that's true but *in* the city nothing can survive. Nobody said anything about out of the city." He chuckled if I didn't remind myself why I was here I would have probably giggled and twirled a strand of loose hair.

I sighed and looked Fredric in the eyes.

"I swear that under different circumstances I would have chosen you, but we can't be together, more or less we can never be. If I had met you in a different life, sure, but then I wouldn't have known you. I'm sorry I have a twisted life but, we can't be."

He nodded, he didn't hide his pain as well as Lewis did.

"One more thing," I said before he could say his goodbyes. "Don't tell the others about this, and tell Robert Gribsom to come here."

More and more men entered and exited this room as the minutes went by. I was so tired I rested my head on the desk and started to sleep.

"Elyon, Elyon. Wake up, love." I felt a slight tapping on my shoulder.

"Shut up alarm clock." I mumbled. I heard a familiar voice chuckle and I immediately got up.

"You know, there is no, and I mean no comparison between me and an alarm clock."

"Seth! Oh my gosh! What are you doing here? Another ones going to be in here any moment now!"

"You mean Darren?" He sat down on top of the desk tracing the pattern in the wood with his index finger.

"Yes, but-"

"You do know he's my brother right?"

"Yes and-"

"So which lucky guy are you going to pick?" He asked lifting my face from my hard stare at the ground.

"I was going to talk to you about that…" I trailed off my voice quivered at each word.

"Don't worry, I already knew this was going to happen years ago, except in that case it was to your sister, of course." I gave a sarcastic laugh and looked at Seth. He seemed so serious. He wanted to know who I had chosen and sadly, I would have to tell him.

"Seth, I love you, if you didn't have this betraying rep I would have picked you, I still do. Seth I have to ask *you* will you marry *me*, Elyon Wuerch, not this fake person I'm pretending to be."

He wrapped his arms around me and I felt tears running from his face to mine and then combining with the ones falling from my eyes.

"Yes, yes, yes. I know that, just tell me who you picked." I bit my lip hard and looked at him.

"O.K, you can't blame me for picking him cause it's

the right choice, even Melanie knew that I would have picked him because Elizabeth already loved-"

"Oh, Elyon, please don't tell me you picked my brother." He gave me one small glance and that was all it took. "Why? Do you know how hurt I feel right now?"

"Yes I do, don't you go asking me if I don't feel ashamed, because I do!" I stared at his furrowed brows and he was probably staring at mine, too.

"I had to pick Darren, because Elizabeth would, because he will take my side immediately when I tell him who I actually am, because I can put my complete trust in him! It's not my fault you're on the Queen's *hit list*!"

"Yes it is! I had to take care of you-" He punched the desk so hard the vibration went to the floor and up to the chair I was sitting on.

"No, it's because *you* fell in love with me, I never made you do that!"

"Oh, so it's my fault you're going to marry my brother now, is that it?"

"Seth you're being unbelievable!"

"I'm the unbelievable one!"

"Ugh! You're acting like a child!" I turned around to face a shelf of books. I heard Seth gasp and then a door closed.

"Wow, you two fight like an old married couple." The familiar voice made me whip my head around.

"Darren?" I looked at the confused face.

"What's this?" he asked walking towards us. Seth jumped off the desk and walked up to Darren.

"Darren, can we talk about this?" Seth asked cornering his brother.

"It seems you already remember *him* completely." Darren called over Seth's shoulder.

I looked down at the ground and cringed. I heard Seth and Darren yelling at each other.

"How much did you hear?" I asked.

Darren stopped talking to Seth turned around to look at me. "How much did you hear?" I repeated. Darren furrowed his brows but in a questioning way.

"I walked in on the part where you *had* to pick me."

"Oh, that one." Seth said looking out the window. "I'll leave you two alone."

"Right, you'll probably walk in and obviously we won't know it!" Darren called after him as Seth exited the room.

"What do you mean 'we *wouldn't* know'?" I asked

"I thought you'd know already," he said walking towards the window.

"No, I don't." I said getting out of the chair and walked to his side.

"His power is invisibility."

"Oh." I looked out the window to gaze at the beautiful starry night. The view reminded me so much of the beautiful painting by Vincent Van Gogh, my favourite artist. I laughed at the reality of the statement. Darren turned and raised an eyebrow.

"I was just thinking about the similarities between me and Van Gogh, you know the artist. He is my favourite artist of all time and he was depressed, made beautiful artwork, but was depressed out of his socks.

"I was depressed when Elizabeth left and I kind of still am, well who am I kidding? I'm probably just as bad as him when I think about it. But my life is Seth and Antoinette and with them I have lived, you know?"

Darren bit his lip hard, and licked them once a dark liquid formed from the puncture.

"I'm not Elizabeth if you haven't noticed yet," I said as I continued to stare out the window. "But I know how much you love her," I smirked and turned to him. "It's really not hard to guess. I'm sorry I hurt you, making you think that I *was* my sister-"

"You're Elyon?" he gasped.

"I thought you would have guessed earlier, but yes, yes I am."

"That explains Seth." He said hitting his head. "How could I have been so stupid, you're the only reason he would *ever* walk in the walls of this castle."

"Really, he would do this only for me?" I asked but I realized that I should just be quiet after Darren gave me a pained glance.

"I need you to marry me, well not me, pretend that I'm Elizabeth. You see the Queen *is* evil, Darren. You need to help me so I can stop her. Do you know what she has planned?"
"You just don't get it, do you?" he asked shaking his head. "The Queen won't *let* me leave because of your boyfriend out there." He gestured towards the door.

"I know that the Queen is trying to take over the Faery Dimension. I know she is going to try to kill you too and she already tried to kill Elizabeth. Do you think after that I would *want* to stay here?"

My mouth slipped open and he closed it for me with his hand

"Darren, I-"

"I'll sacrifice myself for Elizabeth's sister any day." And he kissed my forehead. I placed the metal-rose, golden ring in the palm of his hand. He immediately put it on his left hand ring finger and smiled.

We walked towards the door and it opened by itself. It revealed Seth leaning against the threshold.

"Get your hands off my woman, bro." He said with a smirk and nodded towards the arm around my waist. I went to Seth's side and wrapped my arms around him. "Remember, you are *fake* marrying her."

"Wouldn't have it any other way, bro." Darren said and shook Seth's hand.

Chapter 13

Re-Scheduled

"UGH!" I screamed at the top of my lungs. Darren came running into my room at top speed.

"What's wrong, El, what happened?" Darren asked, lifting the pillow off of my face. I frowned at him but I appreciated the new nickname, it was universal for me and Elizabeth.

"Ask Mel!" I yelled grabbing the pillow back from him and falling onto my bed again.

"Melanie?" Darren asked, turning to face Mel who was leaning against the fireplace.

"All I did was tell her she was having a wedding party." I heard Darren groan.

"I thought today was supposed to be her day of rest, though." he asked sitting down next to me.

"At least someone's on my side!" I yelled into the pillow. I could almost feel Mel's eyes roll behind my back.

"Well change of plans, I invited Elizabeths friends over for tea." Mel said walking towards the grand bed.

"I don't even know them, though!" I screamed again, Darren patted my back.

"Am I allowed to come?" Darren asked looking at Mel.

"Sorry but no, Darren. It's an all women party."

"You can't make me go! I won't let you!"

"You know, El, you can't always get your way." Darren said as he carried me off to the ballroom where my pre-wedding party was to take place.

"Hmph." I propped my face in my hand. Darren had forcefully removed me from my room by swinging me over his shoulder, Mel helped too when I wouldn't let myself through the door, of course.

Melanie opened the door for Darren and he carried me into the room. Six girls sat around a circular table in the middle of the ballroom. Three looked like regular girls; one looked younger than me with platinum, short blonde hair and pale skin. The other two were tan, one with golden hair and the other with brown. Another had ice blue skin and purple hair tied up in a bun. The last two had fiery red hair and massive wings.

"Awe, isn't that... adorable!" they all chimed as I entered. I blushed and tucked my head into Darren's chest. Darren gave a chuckle and then let me down.

"Sorry ladies, but this one here won't let me stay." Darren said pointing to Mel, she rolled her eyes but then clapped her hands together.

"So, you all know the saying about starting parties!"

Darren left and I grabbed a seat at the table. Everyone brought presents even though Mel had told them not to. The presents were not the same presents as you'd get for some pre-wedding party on Earth. The blender, furniture, anything that's on your list, really. The presents they bought for *Elizabeth* were the most beautiful jewellery I had ever seen, clothes which were vintage yet modern and other amazing things.

"Thanks so much again, girls. Everything is so amazing. Darren's going to love everything, too."

"We always knew you two would be together," said the tanned blonde named Megret.

"Yeah, it was love at first sight for you two." said the tanned brunette whos name was Grace. She and Megret were fraternal twins and the platinum blonde was their younger sister. Her name was Cornelia. They were all Dryads, forest women, well except for Cornelia she still was a Nymph, a forest *girl*.

"I love how you broke the royalty rule and just picked the guard who you loved! Power to you my friend." One of the fire-head girls said. Their names were Tally and Tori, but I didn't know the difference between each of them.

"Thanks." I said kind of feeling embarrassed.

"So, tell us Darren's reaction when you asked him if he would marry you!" The ice girl exclaimed she was called Calypso; she was from Ice so her name was just a really bad translation.

"Well, umm…" I tried to remember the night before but everything was just a blur. Seth took me to the garden again and we spent the night- I mean morning there. I didn't get a whole lot of sleep but Seth made me feel better.

"He kind of asked me in a way. He said he would sacrifice himself for me any day." A sigh escaped the mouths of everyone.

"That's so romantic." Cornelia's pixie voice chirped. I smiled at her and she blushed, her pale cheeks turning cherry red.

"You know, I think Darrens *the one*." Calypso said stirring her tea. "He seems to be everything you need."

"I'd kill for someone like that." said Tally, or was she Tori?

"You mean literally speaking, Tal." So that was Tori who just spoke, but I knew that I'd forget the slight difference sooner or later. "Did you actually scream at *Ian Myder* to ask you out?" asked Megret, wide eyed.

"Yeah she did I was there and everything!" exclaimed Tori who leaned far forward, almost knocking over a candle. "Whoops!" she giggled picking it up again.

"Remind me to make Elizabeth hang out with some of my friends and see how she survives." I whispered to Mel who laughed. The other girls didn't notice though. They were talking about this Ian person who they treated like a celebrity.

"Well, we better get going, Pixie here has organ lessons." said Grace pointing to Cornelia.

"Hey! You looked like this once!" she exclaimed gesturing to her petite body and her fragile limbs. I examined her whole body now that she was standing and she was really thin, and I mean *thin*. She had absolutely no fat on her, she was just bones. Her cheek bones poked out of her face awkwardly and her hips and knees looked out of place.

I looked at her sisters, Megret was the curviest but Grace was the tallest. Other than that they looked like models for some swimsuit magazine. Their eyes were beautifully big and their lips were naturally dark red and full. Their nails were long and their shoulders, broad.

I couldn't actually believe that they were real people for a second. Teachers always told us in health class that nobody could walk with a body like that and have a healthy lifestyle. But here they were, standing in front of me as radiant as possible.

I gazed back at Cornelia and felt sorry for her. Her sisters were unbelievably beautiful and she was still in that awkward stage of life. I wouldn't have ever been able to stand an older sister, but I always would have wanted one, so I was lucky, I had a twin. Who disappeared and might be dead, but hey, I still had a twin sister.

Slowly everyone left. The last one to leave was Calypso. She seemed really nice and she was the only one who was already married, so she gave me some tips that were helpful, or would have been if I was getting married to Seth.

I sighed and looked at Mel who was cleaning up. She hadn't said a whole lot during the party but now she was in her happy place, cleaning.

"So, which one of them is my maid of honour?" I asked sitting down on a loveseat propped against the back wall.

"None of them actually." Mel said continuing her sweeping.

"What? Who is she supposed to be, then?" I asked.

"She *was* supposed to be you; I don't think that's going to work out, though." I stared wide eyed at Mel. "So I guess you can pick one of them, even though the Queens going to be suspicious, but still technically you don't *remember* Elyon." She smiled at my little cover.

"I don't know, I really like Calypso and Cornelia but…"

"But what?"

"*But* maybe you could be my maid of honour?" I gave a weak smile to Mel who was leaning against the broom.

"You can't be serious."

"It *would* make sense. You have been really helpful the last few days and the Queen has seen that, so if I chose you, she'd understand the obvious reasons."

"But still," Melanie looked at the ground. "A sylph maid being your maid of honour?"

"It makes sense when you think about it. Sylph maid, maid of honour." I smiled

"El… I don't know." I smiled to myself when I realized Mel had caught on to my new nickname. She continued, "Why don't you pick Calypso or something I really don't think this is a good choice."

"But I want you to be there with me! If I start crying instead of saying 'I do' I need you to be there for me!"

"You won't do that."

"I'll do it on purpose if you won't be my maid of

honour." Mel sighed and looked up from the floor with a smirk on her face.

"El, you're such an -" Mel was interrupted as Darren walked in with an enormous cardboard box.

"What the hell?" I let my voice trail off as Darren started opening it. As he dug his nails through the tape the box fell apart and revealed a beautiful wedding dress.

"Who?" I asked. Darren leaned against the mannequin that wore the beautiful wedding dress.

"Guess." Darren said in a sharp voice. I gasped and so did Mel.

"How is the Queen reacting to this?" Mel asked examining the dress.

"She's trying to trace it, to find out where it came from, and she's going on about how she'll send him to jail and then me."

"He's such a boy sometimes." I said looking at the dress.

"Your boyfriends got taste though." Mel said nudging my arm.

"Well I really don't care if this is the most beautiful dress I've seen," Darren said, his tone icy. "Seth knew his boundaries and he should have stuck to them."

"Darren, this is really hard for him, just let him have some of his crude fun." I said holding his hand; I would have expected him to shake it off but he squeezed it tighter.

"I understand that but still he's going to get us all killed!" I rolled my eyes and wrapped my arms around him.

Darren was a great friend and I knew where he's

coming from about how Seth shouldn't get involved. I couldn't imagine how I would feel if Elizabeth started getting involved, A. it would hurt me and B. the queen would probably kill us- more because she's the one who *was* supposed to get married.

"Well, go try it on so I can pretend that Mel got it for you, and please tell me it doesn't fit." Darren said.

"Good luck with that wish. Remember Seth has practically *lived* with me my whole life. I doubt that he'd get a little detail like my size wrong." I said giving Darren a playful punch.

"Hey, a guy like me can hope, right?" he said smiling with only one side of his mouth, the way Seth always smiled.

Mel brought me back to my room with a cart filled with all the presents I had received.

Once we got back, I almost immediately tried on the dress. It was absolutely stunning. It was a very light peach and the left strap was made out of real flowers which flowed randomly along. Then an opening at the bottom had another pattern of flowers flowing down. I stared in awe at it.

"It is beautiful, isn't it?" Mel said walking towards me.

"Oh, Seth..." My eyes started tearing. I couldn't imagine how much pain he must have been in.

"He loves you a lot, doesn't he?" she asked patting my back as tears drained out of my eyes. "After all this is said and done you two can be together, and I can't wait until *that* wedding." Her words were comforting but they made me cry harder. "Now don't get that dress dirty, or Seth will truly be angry."

I slipped out of the dress and decided to go for a horse ride in the forest. The queen said I could if I was accompanied by a guard; her first choice was Darren, naturally.

I got onto Night who I hadn't seen in I-don't-know-how-many-days. It felt nice to ride him again; it seemed he was the only living thing that has been there for me in my greatest time of need.

"That's a nice horse you got there." Darren said as he rode a dark brown horse named Earth.

"Thanks, it's actually Elizabeth's, though." I said giving a weak smile.

"I thought I had seen him before." Darren mumbled.

"Night's a great horse, I'm so happy I had the honour to ride him. When I was riding here he immediately adjusted to me, he's just awesome."

"Just awesome?" Darren asked at my awkward phrase. I shrugged and I picked up my speed to a gallop. Darren instantaneously followed, I looked back over my shoulder and he was laughing but shaking his head.

"You want to race?" He shouted.

"You're on!" I called over my shoulder and I picked up speed. The trail we were on had lots of twists and turns but the dirt had been ridden on so many times it was as if we were running on a sidewalk.

Soon enough Darren had passed me and turned his horse around to block my path. Night skidded to a halt and sent me flying over his head. I screamed but landed in Darrens lap.

He started laughing and I joined in, too. I hadn't had this much fun in years and I couldn't stop laughing.

"Take a breath, El, you're going to knock yourself out!" he laughed. I tried to breathe but just kept on laughing my head off, soon my stomach didn't like laughing this long and I stopped.

Darren kissed my forehead and I gazed at him questioningly. "What did you do that for?" I asked. He held my hand and smiled.

"You're one of the nicest people I have ever met, it's nice to finally meet you and not have to wonder. You're not like your sister at all, and I like that about you."

"Just because we look a-like doesn't mean we are." I said punching his arm lightly. "I even tried to make myself not look like her."

"And what do you mean by that?" he asked.

"Oh yeah, that's right, you haven't seen what *I* look like! Well, usually I wear five pounds of make up, I have bangs, I straighten my hair or pull back in a pony tail, and I have dyed my hair, red, orange, black, brown and green."

"Green?" Darren asked, running his fingers through my blonde wavy hair.

"That was only for a week. Me and my friends went to the *Green Day* concert and we thought it would be kind of cool if, you know, we dyed our hair, so we did."

"What colour is your hair now, I mean if you didn't look like Elizabeth?"

"A really ugly brown, I'm actually happy that my hairs blonde again."

"I liked the colour," I whipped my head around and sent my hair flying into Darrens face. Darren sputtered and then groaned.

"Can you just take a chill pill and not have to see El every five minutes?" Darren asked as I jumped off the horse and ran into Seth's embrace.

"Wouldn't you if Elizabeth was here?" he said as he kissed my forehead. "When you only live for one person shouldn't you spend your life with them?"

"Not when you're called a traitor for hanging out with that person." Darren mumbled, I tried to ignore the comment but it stuck in my mind. Seth waved Darren away as he pulled me towards him for a kiss.

"I can't leave," Darren continued. "She has to be escorted by a member of the guard, Beatrix's orders *and* Mel's."

"I am a guard, heck, I was the *head* guard. You were the one who joined the family business," Seth smirked as he looked up at Darren.

"You probably don't want to be around me so you can go if you want. But I have some news to tell you, things from *in*side the castle where you can't hear anything."

"What news?" I asked pulling away from Seth.

"I know what Beatrix's plan is for you're coronation, *now* slash wedding."

"She's putting them together!" I asked, how much torture does she think I can handle?

"That's not even half of it." Seth said looking down at the ground.

"What is she planning to do, Seth?" Darren asked his tone completely serious.

"When you two are to switch rings the Queen has something in store for Elyon. The ring you shall give her is going to be poisoned. Ely's going to drop dead and it's going to look like you did it. You'll be sent to the dungeons and the Queen shall be queen, forever."

"What?" Darren and I asked at the same time, Seth only nodded.

"We have to do something!" Darren said. Seth shrugged.

"I don't know what we can do. We could switch the rings but then Beatrix will probably pull out a knife and do the job herself." I shivered and saw the truth in the statement.

"We have to prove to the public that she's evil. Wait, how is she going to be Queen forever when these are her last years? She's like 500 or something?" Darren asked.

"She's going to turn herself into ice, the elemental, anyway. So she can live eternity in her prime, you know how women are." Seth nudged me. I was still in shock from the fact that the Queen was going to kill me tomorrow. It's not a situation I take lightly. Before it seemed almost avoidable but now it was inevitable.

"She's going to kill me, she *will* succeed." I whispered. Darren held my hand while Seth still had his arms around me. Darren was now at my side and off of Earth.

"No she won't, not if the Ledger Brothers have anything to do with it, right Dare?" Seth asked smiling.

"Right, Se." Darren laughed at Seth's shortened name and the two of them did this corny-handshake-thingy which I couldn't help but laugh at.

"You two are truly brothers." I laughed. I was so glad that they put aside their troubles to make me happy.

"Can't wait to see yours and Elizabeth's handshake, now." Darren said patting my back. I forced a laugh but Seth didn't bother responding. He knew me and Elizabeth never had a handshake or secret nicknames; he was the one who invented Liz and Ely in the first place.

"Me and Mel will figure out something," Darren said jumping onto his horse. He started riding down the trail but turned around after a moment right before the point where he'd be out of sight. "Oh and Seth,"

"Yes, Dare?" Seth asked. I laughed at the way Seth asked that, almost as if he was saying 'yes, *dear*'.

"Remember to bring her back *before* dawn?" Darren asked raising an eyebrow, the one thing Seth was incapable of.

"Of course, Dare." I had to laugh again and Seth pulled me closer towards him. Then Darren rode off mumbling something about how Seth was pushing his buttons.

Chapter 15

Goodbyes

Everything was happening too fast and I just wanted it all to stop. I wanted everything to go backwards so I could right anything I did wrong, which was practically my whole life. I also wanted everything to go forwards, though. To get past this mountain of a problem.

I realized I was a very egotistical person who only cared about themselves. I blamed everything on everyone's else and thought I was some perfect child screwed up by everyone else in my life. I realized what I wanted didn't matter. Not even what I needed mattered, anymore.

I'd ask for a glass of water and people would say be quiet. I'd ask for some spare change to pay the difference at the grocery store but they said tough love. I realized what mattered was what others needed, others who actually needed it.

Some people, and I mean people who never actually

knew me, looked at me and said 'what a poor girl' or 'I don't know how I could live in a situation like that' didn't understand that I was just being lazy, I didn't help others at the time so I couldn't help myself.

Now when I actually *could* help some people out, there was another blocking my view of them. This person was Beatrix. The people who I needed to help were everyone. It seems like the odds are in my favour but you never truly know if that's true or not.

I have read many books in my lifetime and when the main character is about to die you look at how many more pages of the book are actually left, and most of the time there's a whole lot left, which to me is a little bit of hope. Hope that maybe I'll come out of this day alive.

*

"Mel, I can't breathe." I said sitting down again.

"You're going to ruin the dress," she yelled at me, "for the fifty millionth time!" I wasn't helping her out by being this stubborn.

"But I'm going to faint." I said closing my eyes and rubbing my forehead. She pulled me back up and put the finishing touches on the dress. "Where's Darren?" I asked panting.

"He's probably in the hall. You can't see him though!" I knew that it was bad luck or something rather if the groom saw the bride in her wedding dress before the wedding but I didn't love Darren, so did it actually matter?

"El," Melanie began taking my hand in hers. She looked stunning in her plain off-white dress. It had a square neck and thick straps and it showed her knees. My other maids in the same dress were Calypso and Cornelia. I debated if this would make Megret and Grace jealous but it would make Cornelia happy that she got to be a part of something and her beautiful sisters didn't.

"You just have to do this. You promised me you wouldn't do anything stupid. I expect you to keep that promise."

At that moment the door swung wide open but nobody walked in. It slammed shut and then almost a second later Seth appeared. Mel smiled and mouthed 'thank you' to him. She respected the idea of him being at the wedding, not like Darren who was appalled by it.

"Seth," I cried and lunged myself into his arms.

"You look more than beautiful in that dress, do you like it?" he asked his voice soft but it cracked at the end and I held him tighter to hope that he wouldn't start crying.

"I love it almost as much as I love you." I said taking two gulps of air.

"I'll leave you two alone." Mel said slipping away out of the door.

"I don't know if me seeing you like this will affect our wedding or if it won't." Seth said smiling.

"How can you be so sure that we'll live through this day? Oh yeah, the Queen's not trying to kill *you*!"

"Elyon, I know we can pull this off. I'll be right there. I love you; I have never loved anyone else because I was waiting for *you* to give me a chance." Seth bit his lip. He then took my hand and sat me down.

"All those guys you'd bring to your house and I'd be there waiting to interrogate them, it wasn't only cause I wanted you to have a good guy or to keep you safe but to prove to you that they weren't the one you wanted." My mouth was opened a little and I couldn't believe what I was hearing.

"I'm the one who didn't notice *you*." I silently whispered to myself. I remembered all those songs I had written, talking about how some guy I liked didn't even know I existed, but *I* was the one who ignored Seth.

"That's what I've been trying to show you your whole life!" Seth said his eyes starting to tear.

"Don't cry, Seth, don't." I said burying my face into his chest. He kissed my head. I heard him sniffle back his tears and he pulled away to look at me.

"I'll be right there in the pews, you don't have to worry about anything, nothing at all." Seth walked towards the door.

"Wait, Seth!"

"Yes?"

"I love you, goodbye." I said as tears slipped down my cheeks. His face looked pained but mine was probably worse. He shook his head and turned invisible.

The door opened by the Invisible Man and then closed leaving me by myself which almost killed me right there and then.

"Breathe El; remember this will be over in five seconds." Mel said patting my back.

I stood in the vestibule holding flowers, flower girls, my maids and everyone else stood in front of me. The Queen stood beside me holding my hand.

I nodded at Mel but I couldn't say anything, holding back tears.

The music started playing and I couldn't breathe at all. Everyone started walking and I followed mechanically. I saw Darren and he gave a small wave. I smiled and everything seemed to be better. I found my breath and proceeded in walking down the aisle.

I was almost up the stairs when my eyes caught on someone. I could perfectly see Seth sitting in the front row beside Tally and Tori. My breath caught and the Queen patted my back thinking that I was choking. She followed my gaze and Seth *waved* at me. He put his finger over his mouth as a sign to tell me to be quiet. I swallowed hard and proceeded up the stairs.

The queen let go of my hand and stood in between Darren and I.

"Inhabitants of NorthStar, it is my honour and great pleasure to mark this day the beginning of our new ruler Elizabeth Wuerch!" The audience clapped and I heard some cheers, then the congregation fell silent.

"We shall wed Miss Wuerch to Darren Ledger today; he shall be her consort for ruling this land!" The ceremony went on.

I had never been to a wedding before but what people say about them being boring is true. Well first off faery weddings seem relatively the same as human weddings as far as I know from my movie and TV show knowledge, except that there's *a lot* more talking. The Queen just went on and on how we will rule together for the end of time, and blah, blah blah, blah blah.

When I was supposed to say 'I do' even though I rehearsed it more than five *million* times I said 'yes'.

Oh I am the biggest idiot on earth! And now in the faery dimension, too. No one made a big deal out of it anyway, which made me feel loads better, but still…

The Queen looked far back and called out at the top of her lungs: "Bring out the rings!" I caught my voice so I wouldn't let out a scream. Seth, who I had been staring at the entire wedding gave me a painful expression and blew me a kiss. I held my breath again and Darren grabbed my hand which was hidden behind the Queen.

It's going to be okay. He mouthed; I nodded but didn't look at him.

Tally and Tori came up with both rings. The rings were gold with black spirals that moved with each step they took.

It was easy to tell which one was for me and which one was for Darren. Mine had the spirals spinning in directions that spelled out *Queen Elizabeth 7th Queen of NorthStar*. Darrens only spiralled in the direction of his name, nothing fancy.

The Queen took the box which held the rings and held it up for everyone to see. She smiled at them and then turned towards me. Her smile changed into something cruel and vile; I shivered and looked toward Seth for help. He furrowed his brows in a questioning way since he couldn't raise one. I guess he couldn't see the Queens face with her back turned against him.

The Queen turned to Darren and knelt down on both knees.

"King Darren, if you will slip the ring on your wife's finger and proceed through the coronation." She bowed her head on the last few words and I saw Seth from the corner of my eye tilting his head to see the Queens face.

Why hadn't he been caught yet? He was sitting in bloody plain sight! My heart started beating faster and my ring glowed bright as though it wasn't a ring but a star in the box.

Darren bit his lip and frowned while observing the task at hand.

"Queen Beatrix, your majesty, wouldn't it be more commendable if you placed the ring on the future queens finger? It makes sense when you think about it, I mean, passing the ring from one generation to the next, from one queen to the other, this new tradition could be well passed on for generations if we practice it now."

I raised my eyebrow at Darren and mouthed *what the hell are you doing?* The Queen had the same expression on her face, but Seth smiled and laughed *The Ledger Bro's survive, viva la hermano!* I actually didn't even know how I could read all those words from his lips.

The congregation seemed to like the idea though, heads nodded and many cheers roared through the crowd.

Darren smiled and cheered: "Who's with me?" the audience again cheered and a smile crept on my face. The Queen growled at Darren but he shrugged.

"We aren't following the rules anyway. Who has had a wedding and a coronation at the same time?" he asked smiling.

"I still don't know if that's best." The Queen shivered.

"I think it's a great idea." I suggested; my voice

unbelievably believable. Beatrix stared me down but sighed.

"Fine but everyone knows that *Darren* was supposed to put the ring on your finger, remember that." She said a little too loud. I gulped knowing the meaning behind those words.

She took the ring and sighed. "Queen Elizabeth the seventh queen of NorthStar, do you agree to balance the unbalanced magic and agree to all the conditions that you may have to go through to become the proper queen for the second Faer city of all time."

"I do." I said solemnly.

"Very well then." She slipped the ring on my finger and once she released her hand from mine in a never ending grace, I fell to the ground.

My eyes stayed open and they seemed to freeze. No tears and no dry eyes. I felt myself shaking though, and the cold hard floor didn't help the pain from the fall. But the main feeling in my entire body was the golden ring on my finger; a small little pulse came from my veins under it. I could feel the spirals slow as my heart beat did the same.

I wasn't paying attention to the congregation but I heard screams gasps and people already accusing Darren, which really hurt me. I felt like I should have cried, I felt like I should have yelled sorry at the top of my lungs but I couldn't make myself. My voice couldn't even escape my lips or come up my throat. I could see the Queen hovering over me through my glazed eyes but I didn't look at her. I continued staring my dazed eyes at the ceiling. She then stood up and bellowed in a loud scripted voice.

"You! You did this! To your... your queen! I can't believe it Darren, I thought you were different! It turns out you're only a replica of your brother!" Darren stalked towards her his face raged with anger.

"Never talk about my brother like that, and I am not his twin! I am not his clone! I am me! I make my own decisions and my own choices and he makes his! We are not the same person!" I could hear his breath loud in the now quiet hall.

"You know," I heard footsteps walking up onto the stairs and my breath stopped and so did my heart for a second. "I finally had the guts to walk in these halls and you push your luck, Beat."

"Don't call me that CrossStarian!" the Queen yelled at the top of her lungs. The entire crowd gasped and some shouting insults.

"Well then don't call me CrossStarian; even Stevens."

"You've been with that human girl, Elyon, for too long, when I kill her too everything will be fine." More gasps ran through the crowd, I even felt vibrations on the ground from somebody who had fallen faint, I guess.

"You mean her?" Seth's face came into my view and he held out his hand in front of me. When I stretched out my arm he smiled from ear to ear. He pulled me up and wrapped his arms around me.

"What?" Beatrix asked speechless.

"This here's Elyon, not Elizabeth; we have no clue where that one is." Seth tilted his head to the side.

"That's Elyon! But how...?"

"Because things like these are easy to pull off

when you have an identical twin, like the Olsen's have revealed to the world. Oh, that's right! You don't have cable here." I chuckled.

The Queen still looked like she didn't understand so Seth stood in front of me and his hand glowed blue, he pressed his hand over my heart and I closed my eyes. I felt like a wind was blowing over me, like the windstorms we'd get in Weston. I opened my eyes and the congregation gasped.

"See, you're beautiful being *you*." Seth whispered in my ear. I looked down and could see threads of an ugly shade of brown hanging around my shoulders. I had jeans on, not a beautiful dress anymore, and a tank top. I had my Champion sneakers on which I had since grade six.

I looked up to see Darren smiling "I've been waiting for this," he said walking towards me.

"Beatrix, we knew your little plan to kill El, who you thought was El*izabeth*. Thanks to Seth here. We obviously switched the rings, and I made *you* put the ring on her to show everyone I had nothing to do with the poison. Why would I want to kill my best friend?"

Darren smiled and my heart completely fell out of my body and exploded on the ground, too confused to even know whether to stop beating or to beat uncontrollably.

"You think you can stop my reign? You little punk kids and a human? You thought wrong! Head guard! Show Elyon to the dungeons and dispose of these traitors."

The guards at the back of the room looked at each other confusedly.

"Well?" She asked pointing towards us.

"Beatrix you never got another head guard after Seth left." Darren stated with a smug smile. But that didn't stop the rest of the guard from charging us. They grabbed me by my arms and clasped shackles around my wrists.

"Seth!" I yelled tears *now* deciding to escape my eyes.

"Elyon, don't worry I'm going to save you! Or I *will* die trying!" he yelled as guards attacked him from every corner. I looked at Darren who was fighting off the rest of them with his sword.

"You have to stop this Beatrix! You can't hurt innocent people!" I screamed as people started filing out of the church screaming in horror.

"Oh, you think you're innocent, that's cute. I thought the king made it clear for you to stay away! He was trying to save you, that's why *I* wanted you to come here." She sat down on the thrown, crossing her right leg over her other swinging it there so casually like the first day I met her at the court or when I saw her again while pretending to be Elizabeth.

The guards started pulling me by my forearms, making my legs tangle on the ground.

"Seth! I love you! Save yourself! You're worth way more than I am!" I made eye contact with him and he gave me a pained expression.

"I love you, though." He said and completely stopped fighting. A sword came hard on him but he didn't dodge it in time; it scraped his face, leaving a bloody gash from the corner of his eye through his eyebrow.

"No!" I screamed but I was already out of the church.

"Let go of me!" I yelled as I was forced along a narrow corridor. The walls were grey with some surreal paintings on them, not modern surrealism but originals of some old dead guys.

The guards gave each other a glance and then threw me into a room and slammed the metal door shut.

"Hey!" I yelled banging on the door. "I didn't mean that literally!" I sighed and gave a quick observation of the situation I seemed to be stuck in.

I was in a pitch black room and I could only see the fingers in front of me. There was a small window on the far wall right up to the ceiling, sealed with iron bars.

I sighed again and trudged towards the wall with the window. It was obvious I was in the dungeon, there was no doubt about that, but something about that fact didn't make me feel any better.

"I'm going to die here; I'm sure as hell going to die here." I said out loud. I doubted anyone could hear me so why would they care if I was going crazy and talking to myself.

"All I ever wanted was a normal life. I didn't want to be involved with this *ever*. I guess my mother was trying to help me with that but failed to do so without getting rid of her other daughter.

"Now Seth is going to have to suffer just like Darren. The Queen is going to try to over throw Fate and all will be hectic. I should just give up; yell to the guards 'hey I give up just send me back home!' Sadly, things just don't work that way." I rested my head against the wall and then slowly slipped down it until I was a puddle of Depressed Elyon.

I tried to close my eyes but the darkness stayed the same and the darkness scared me so I decided to keep my eyes open.

It isn't easy to sleep with your eyes open but I couldn't stand closing them for a second, possibly scared that maybe they wouldn't open ever again. I was ready to just disappear but dying still made me nervous.

But I continued to try, and continued to talk to myself, not bothering to whisper my thoughts in my mind. I felt myself almost fall asleep when I saw something move in the shadows.

The light flickered from the window and to the other side of the room. But the light stayed in the other corner, a wave of golden light. The strange radiance in the room made me shiver but I pretended to ignore it.

"My friends weren't really my friends, well, Charlie, Mandy and Leslie anyway. I only had Antoinette and Seth, and I guess now Darren, but that's about it. Even when Elizabeth *was* here, she never completely paid attention to me, just stupid Beatrix."

"You really think that?" I whipped my head to the streak of light and realized it was just the sunlight beaming off of a lock of hair.

My breath caught and I looked at the source of the high-pitched voice. There sat a small girl, very fair and had light blonde hair. She had very large eyes for such a small face and thin pink lips, but the thing that I was afraid of the most was that she had massive butterfly styled wings. She looked so fragile though, as if she would fall apart if you blew on her.

"I said," she repeated, clearing her soft-high voice. "Do really think I never paid attention to you? Do you *think* that's the truth?"

My eyes bulged out of my face as I squinted in the obscurity.

"El, I mean... Elizabeth?" my voice cracked half way through, I could almost swear I was just dreaming.

"No, I'm some prisoner here," said the girl rolling her eyes.

"How did you... are you captured here also?" I asked astonished.

"Obviously not, or I would be in chains like you." she nodded towards my handcuffed wrists. I frowned, annoyed at her tone. "I came to see you; obviously Seth wasn't doing his job well enough lately, so I needed some, reinforcements, and by that I mean myself."

"You're not Elizabeth; you're rude; that's what you are!" I said. She sighed and walked over towards me taking a seat.

"Well, I can't say anything different for you of course, 'I didn't pay any attention to you' yeah that's *so* true."

"Can you stop with the sarcasm, that's my talent, not yours?" I gave a weak laugh trying to realize that this was my sister beside me, but for some reason I just couldn't grasp it.

"Fine, but you have to answer my question." she said laughing her small quiet giggle which seemed to hurt to listen to. I sighed but I wasn't going to rephrase my answer. Why should I when she never thought about my feelings before?

"You only talked about Beatrix and you never really

played with me. You'd only go on about your fantasy world." I said staring her in the eye. Elizabeth was never serious; I had to make her usually.

"That hurt right there," she said curling herself into a small ball. "Can we talk about something else? What have you done while I was living *fantasy world*?" She asked using hand motions, the way she did even as a little girl.

"Well, Antoinette also was hurt by your sudden absence. She was your friend too, you know. I failed school, Mom put me in all these activities, trying to get my mind off of you, and Charlie became evil." I took a deep breath trying to remember that I wanted to be nice to Elizabeth.

"I can't say I had that much fun either," She started resting her small head on my shoulder. It felt awkward but I let her stay. "I stayed with the Queen until I realized she was trying to kill me, I only told Melanie and Seth that I was running away. Seth came with me but Darren got the wrong impression and…"

"Yeah, I know how that feels." I said sighing. "Pretending to love Darren hurt Seth so much; I don't even know how he survived."

"Anyways, I left to CrossStar, where I stayed for a little bit and then I wanted to go back to Weston to see you but Seth wouldn't let me. We got into this big fight and… and I hurt him. That night I completely changed, I wasn't the Elizabeth everyone knew and loved, I was this evil version, worse than you ever were."

"Thanks." I said patting her head mockingly.

"Don't mention it." Elizabeth sighed. "I left CrossStar, hiding my face from every citizen. I lived in the Un-named Forest for years until you came. I was so happy, hoping you could set me free from the self driven curse I put on myself. And you did. I love you Elyon."

She wrapped her arms around me and smiled wildly in my face. Her whole mood swung at full speed and turned the other way, giving me whip lash.

"I missed you, Liz, never leave me again, do you understand that? Never get lost in some evil world which ends up ruining... our life." I immediately thought of Seth and Darren. It was pretty funny the little sibling with sibling relationship I had gotten myself into.

"Trust me." she said. Hiding her face from the sunlight that had crept in, behind my back.

"So about the wings thing, when the hell did *that* happen?"

"Well, if you had stuck with the coronation-"

"You mean if I had died?"

"Fine, *if Beatrix didn't want to kill you then,* you would've had to take a Queens Test, they call it, I took it, became a faery then the Queen tried to kill me and now I'm here. You probably know the whole story off by heart now, am I right?"

"I could probably recite it on the P.A system at school, that's how well I know it. Though I don't want to be able to do that." I mumbled with a weak smile.

I sighed and stared into the darkness, I didn't want Elizabeth here, I realized. It seemed she's the reason why my life sucks so why should I love her. I started to heat up and Elizabeth let go of me.

"Ely...?"

"Where were you?" I asked her my tone sharp. In

that second she turned into the Elizabeth I used to know.

"Excuse me?"

"You didn't go deaf when you became a faery did you? I asked you a simple question: where were you when I was falling to pieces? You ruined my life Elizabeth, and you can never change that! Even if somehow I and Seth survive this I still will never be the happy little girl I used to be! Wait; scratch that, when I was a little girl I had a sister who didn't even know who I was!"

My throat ached after screaming at her so loudly.

"Watch me help you. I owe my life to you Elyon. I shall either die of old age or *you* will have to kill me. Watch me save your life, *right now.*"

"And how, may I ask, are you going to do that?" I asked, matter-o-factly.

"Watch." She stood up and closed her eyes. She mumbled something and then she disappeared. I looked around the room but couldn't find her. Of course, I *was* only dreaming. I sighed of relief but something inside of me felt pained.

"Liz…?"

I felt a light tap on my shoulder. "I'm right here." I heard a loud gruff voice whisper. I whipped my head around and stared at a tall, very muscular guard.

"What the hell?"

"I'll explain later." He or she, I don't know! The guard said, clasping a large hand around my mouth.

The guard walked to the door and started banging wildly on the bars.

"Let me out of here! You incompetent dimwits!" I heard many footsteps run towards the gate.

"Oh sorry Manny, uh how did *that* happen, Jones?" I saw two guards open the door to let out the one trapped in here; I started realizing what was happening.

As the door closed shut with a whisper, I heard a loud punch and I saw one bloody-nosed guard fall to the ground. The other stood wide-eyed in horror as another punch flew to his face.

The gate opened again and I saw Elizabeth smile.

"I won't say 'I told you so' if you say thank you." She said a little smugly.

"Thanks holy-cows much." I said running towards the door.

We darted down the hallways at top speed; faster than I had ever ran before. Elizabeth was laughing the whole time, sprinting made her happy so she told me, and sprinting with *me* made her feel 'on cloud nine'.

"So…you can shape shift, is that it?" I asked my breath heavy as I ran.

"Uhuh, for us, whatever affect your human life has on you affects your special talent in the Faery world. I've always wanted to be like you. It's the only reason I tried so hard to stay the same and move back to Weston. So I received the gift of shape shifting, makes sense when you think about it.

I was silent for a moment. You could only hear my breath coming out hoarsely out of my lungs.

"You wanted to be like me?" My lips barely moved as I whispered.

"Yeah, you could almost say that you were my role model." I just straightened out my thoughts but they acted like an elastic band and just snapped back at me.

"Can't say the same thing for myself though," I

sighed, "I dyed my hair and did everything almost rebel-like to *not* be like you. I didn't want to have anything to do with you. I'm sorry."

My voice cracked at the end and I started to slow my run as I waited for a reply from Elizabeth. But nothing came out of her mouth. I looked at her, taking my hard gaze away from the ground.

"There's only one way you'll succeed in saving Seth and the kingdom, now." She alleged while changing the subject. "You must first defeat the King, a sissy and then the Queen. Do not, and I repeat, *do not* kill the Queen. She is the only heir for Glacée, the Ago Planet, so you mustn't kill her."

"Ok, I'll so ignore that subject change if you tell me how to fight." I completely stopped running and waited for her to argue with me.

"Ugh, you have to get a *sword* since a faery can wipe you out in a second if you only use your hands." She stopped a little farther up the hall but didn't bother walking towards me.

"Now where the hell am I supposed to get one of those?" I asked. I didn't even know how to use a sword. The only time I had ever held one was in grade 4 when my teacher brought one in for our medieval unit.

"Seth probably has one on him so just find him and you'll be alright." She grabbed my arm in a quick second and dragged me as she ran even *faster* than before, completely lifting me off of the ground.

We stopped, finally, in front of a small window, as large as the one in the jail cell. I shook my head but Elizabeth cracked open the bars with one pull of her delicate hands and pushed me through.

On the other side of the wall was chaos, absolute chaos.

A few swords lay randomly on the ground along with five million dead soldiers and another five million dead rebel soldiers from CrossStar.

The sight of this made me queasy but Elizabeth caught me when my knees were about to buckle.

"Just watch me." She lifted herself off the ground and flew in circles around everyone.

She was only a fast moving blue and golden streak-like when I saw her in the Un-named Forest. She soared through the air and would descend on enemies; killing them in one swift stroke.

At first I gagged and almost vomited on the battle grounds but after I stood in awe. She was no longer the little girl I remembered. She was my equal, and she had finally grown up.

"Yeah like I can do that." I responded as she sat right down beside me. She was about to say something but a guard who was at the wedding had spotted us and was running towards our direction.

Elizabeth dashed towards him and with one blow of her fist; he was clutching the side of his face, down on the ground.

"Go!" She yelled from a distance as she battled four more guards.

I started to run but I didn't know where I was going. I didn't belong on this battlefield; I didn't belong anywhere in fact.

I tried to find Seth, *yes first find Seth then get a sword*, I whispered to myself. I looked up and almost immediately saw him fighting for his life against the King.

"SETH!" I screamed but my voice was too harsh and my throat burned after yelling. He didn't notice me which was odd but I continued to sprint to him.

As I got closer someone fell on top of me as they absorbed a strike. The person let out a scream and I realized, he was just a kid, probably no older than 14. My eyes burned as he stared at me, his eyes bloodshot.

"I'm so sorry." I said to him but he didn't understand what I meant. He probably didn't even know who I was.

Nails clasped into my arms as somebody tugged me upwards.

"Hey!" I yelled, but again my voice only came out as a whisper.

"Oh my god, it is you!" Seth said shocked to see me. I wrapped my arms around him and kissed him even though this was a *huge* mistake.

A soldier pushed us over and Seth's arm got squashed by both of our weight. He let out a scream but immediately got up and attacked the man.

I screamed at the soldier for hurting Seth but another person decided to grab me by the arm and pull me up.

"Child! You should have just stayed in the cellar!" A familiar voice lectured at me.

"Ma Beat?" I asked almost not recognizing her.

"If you want to fight you better know how to!" She yelled over some loud explosion.

"Why aren't faeries using their powers?" I asked

astonished not to see any blue light coming from Seth's palms.

"Because this is a treaty match, it must be even to everyone, including you." She said jabbing one of her fingers in front of my face.

"Me? But I was in the dungeon." I asked befuddled.

"We all knew you'd escape, it's just your personality, Elyon. Even the queen knew when she did it. That's why she didn't lock up Seth or Darren; you would have been out with them even quicker." She gave me a light-hearted punch but then her face turned serious again.

"You're going to need a sword, do you know how to use one?" she interrogated.

"No, who does?" I tilted my head, in shock that everyone seemed to think a sword was just a household object here.

"Ok, magic isn't allowed as an offensive mechanism but no one said I couldn't give you a boost." She lifted her hands to my face and blew a red breath on my eyelids.

"I give you intelligence." She said smiling.

"What did you just do?" I asked wiping away the windblown tears from my eyes.

"I gave you a gift I've been wanting to give you for a long time now. It's my talent." She explained while smiling. "Now go out there and get a sword!" She pushed me towards Seth and the King.

As I walked towards Seth, he pushed me to the ground and I gasped.

"Don't fight! I already almost lost you last time I don't want to lose you again!" He shouted as he continued fighting. I noticed the soldier who attacked us both earlier was lying on the ground, dead.

"Give me a sword, I know how to fight!" I yelled back at him, or it wasn't me yelling at him, it was something inside of me.

I actually *did* know how to fight. He looked at me and then away. I heard him groan as he tossed a sword into the air. I caught it perfectly in thin air which surprised me. I couldn't usually catch a baseball if I wanted to never mind a sword thrown randomly.

As if suddenly I became a threat, guards charged at me in every direction. Right then and there, I made a silent vow that I wouldn't kill anyone, as that wasn't the person I was. So each time someone tried to throw a hatchet at me, first I'd cringe, then second I'd send a gash on their leg from their hip to their shin. Disabling them but *not* killing them.

When I finally got to the King, Seth smiled at my progress and allowed me to take a few blows at him. Of course I let Seth kill the King but before Seth took the sword out of my hands and finally end the King's life, the King spoke.

"Elyon, kill your sister, kill her so she can never rule again. I promise you, if you let her live, she will be more of a menace then ever." He whispered in pain.

"I could never kill her." I replied looking away. And then Seth ended his life.

I was hidden by trees as I fell unconscious. Seth noticed that the Kings words had hurt me and he told me to lay low for a little bit. But I was too restless. Melanie, who was fighting also, gave me a pill that would help me clear my thoughts, a side effect was unconsciousness for fifteen minutes but some sleep would do me well.

In my comatose moments flashes of the battle before scattered through my head before they disappeared. Dead bodies on the ground. Blood everywhere. And small children and women crying in pain as they saw they're loved ones die.

I was in more pain than all of them. The king had asked me to kill my very own sister. I could never do that. Sure it seems she was taking a likely path but to end anyone's life in general to me was almost a certain death for myself. I would never take a life and survive.

As the good memories filled my mind I felt a little more relaxed, they were all mostly of Seth, a few of Antoinette, and one or two of Darren or Mel. I was about to *actually* fall asleep when someone tapped me on the shoulder.

"James?" I asked rubbing my eyes trying to figure out who stood in front of me.

"Hah, you still remember me." He said rubbing tears away from my face. "Have you seen Melanie by any chance? Beatrice told me she was here a few minutes ago."

I smiled remembering that Mel and James were together. They were perfect for each other; that was for sure. He was kind sweet and gentle. And she was humorous and loving.

"She's inside taking cover." I said continuing my smile, boy did that pill work.

"Thanks a lot, Elyon." He started to run away but

I yelled back for him. "Yes?" he asked starting to look anxious.

"She misses you lots, you better still love her." I said in a playful lecturing tone.

"Don't worry about me, ma'am." He smiled sprinting in the battlefield.

I got back up and found my sword was right beside me. I tried to find Seth again, he was my battle partner. But I could only see Elizabeth flying over people and swooping down for them like a pelican. She was the only faery who I had actually seen fly. I wondered why that was but the answer, I knew, wouldn't be revealed until this battle was won.

I spotted the Queen and Seth.

I caught Seth's gaze and smiled widely while waving my hand. I started to run towards them but then the Queen gave a cruel glance from me to Seth.

Seth took a quick punch at her but she dodged it with gracefulness. She took a tall staff that she had in her hands and stabbed Seth's right wing. He cried and dropped to the ground.

My whole body stopped functioning as his eyes closed. I couldn't process what was going on but I ran towards the menace.

I rushed towards her, anger swelling inside of me. "You killed him!" I yelled at her, but she just smiled wickedly. I swung my sword high above me, ready to strike but she pushed me down.

"You fragile little human, you think you can kill me? That's almost pitiful." I roared again and tried to strike her but she dodged. "You silly Elyon, why waste your time on me while you could be saving Seth's life?"

I gasped at the reality of her statement. I should have been mending Seth's wounds. What a bad lover am I? But she was probably just tricking me, waiting to kill *me* herself. Maybe Seth wasn't even dead but those words were only to soothe me. I knew that I was lying to myself.

I tried again to attack her but it seemed someone else beat me to it.

Darren cut off a length of her hair as he rode bareback on Earth. She screamed and turned to throw her staff at him but I was quick on my feet. I banged my sword on the top of her head, knocking her down.

I smiled at Darren who looked impressed. But Darrens face changed in a quick moment.

"Elyon, NO!" But it was too late. Beatrix took her ice like claws and stabbed them into my side. I let out a high-pitched shriek and fell to the ground. This time I wasn't faking.

Everything was turning black though my eyes were still open wide.

Epilogue:
Unknown

Elizabeth

I sat silently in the waiting area. I let my eyes flicker from page to page of a *Seventeen* magazine randomly. Not completely sure which articles I wanted to read or not. They were all about *lover* problems which I had always rolled my eyes to.

I heard a soft click of red glossy high heels clack across the floor. I lifted my nose out of the magazine and then looked at the empty seat beside me.

As I continued to read I saw the red high heels stop in front of me and then sit down.

"You were right." the woman said, no pity or regret in the smallest place of her strong voice.

"I always am." I said, not arrogantly but matter of factly.

"How did you know though, that isn't your gift, is

it?" she asked quietly not the letting the receptionist understand the main topic of our conversation.

"No it isn't, but I knew, every prophesy ever told has said she lives forever, to doubt that all now is crazy and shows lack of faith." I said putting a pair of green square glasses on my face. I liked them a lot, they were Prada, obviously, and it was just too bad that the square rims wouldn't look good on my real face.

"I never said I doubted The Prophesy, Elizabeth!" she said taking the magazine forcefully away from me. She seemed to be annoyed with me, I couldn't help it, it was only my new personality.

"Now, Fate, what would we all do if someone decided that we could only have *one* Queen for The Sky and The Earth, hmm?" I asked taking off my glasses and biting one of the ends, a bad habit which came with this body.

"It doesn't make much sense does it?" I continued. "We need Elyon as much as we need Beatrice and Beatrix. Balance and many rulers is the only way to maintain peace in the Faery Dimension and Earth now." Fate seemed to breathe and I put on my glasses again.

Fate leaned in closer to me and looked at the receptionist who seemed to be interested in our discussion.

"What are going to be the new roles?" She whispered in a snake-like voice. "You and your sister are going to be the hardest."

"I'd prefer Aether, Sky. More freedom and I can't mess up."

"What about consorts? I find it easier to rule alone."

"Well that's kind of going against everything we stand for." I smiled, obviously she wanted to be ruler of the entire Fey Dimension but she could have at least kept her mouth shut; citizens might find out and might discover democracy is the best way to solve everything.

"What I mean is, are you and Darren going to be able to stay with each other?" She whispered even quieter than before. "If you don't have a strong relationship now, imagine how this could effect our world."

"I take offense to that, I'll let you know." I coughed. "Darren and I love each other more than anything, we have been together longer than Elyon and Seth, even." I stated matter-o-factly.

"Yes, but can it stay that way?" Fate asked not bothering to whisper anymore. I was about to respond but I was interrupted by another voice.

"Your... cousin is ready to see you Miss... Perkin." The receptionist called from her desk. I looked up and met eyes with the frail woman. I nodded and excused myself from Fate.

I walked down the hospital hallway and into room 174, where Elyon lay on a hospital bed. She frowned when she saw me at first but I quickly showed her who I *actually* was and she nodded in agreement.

Showing my real identity to the public of Weston would create too much publicity for such a small time-frame I'd be here. I was the town's gossip for a decade, to come back now would ruin Elyon's life even more.

"How are you feeling, Ely?" I asked stroking her head. She smiled stiffly.

"I finally know what's going on around here. That stupid nurse wouldn't tell me anything, not even if Seth was alive! So I went a bit psycho,"

"So I've heard." I mumbled too quietly for her to understand.

"I'm just happy I'm alive and Seth is, too. Also everyone who I attacked. I didn't want to hurt anyone."

"Of course you didn't." I forgot to mumble that one so she tilted her head angrily.

"I thought the rude Elizabeth had moved away to South Africa?" she crossed her arms against her chest but winced at the pain in her side.

"Sorry, I'll admit that was a bit impolite." I smirked. I didn't like lying to my sister, honestly. But it was what I had to do to get her to re-like me. She still thought the quiet imaginative Elizabeth was inside of me but she was wrong. *I have changed* I whispered to myself, *and I am never going back.*

At that moment another person entered the room. I didn't need to turn to see who it was because a large smile had spread across Elyon's face.

"Elyon, Elizabeth." Seth nodded as he walked towards us and kissed Elyon on the forehead.

"Seth." I replied standing up.

Elyon had changed a lot herself since I left her. She actually changed the same way I did but she had Seth with her. He made her happier than anything could possibly. But then she changed *again*. She now was focused on Seth and had restarted her life revolving around him.

I sighed and started out the door. "See you later, Ely." I said quietly.

"Wait!"

I turned around and looked at Elyon. She slumped into her shoulders at my cold stare.

"I just wanted to say…" Elyon began. "You were wrong about CrossStar."

"I already knew that." I said bitterly.

"No, you ignored it as though it wasn't important. *Everything* is important, Liz, never forget that."

I rolled my eyes and walked out the door.

"What was that about?" Elyon asked but I had already slipped out of the door.

I let a nurse cart pass by me before I pressed my ear to the door. I focused hard, trying to channel the words from the other room to my ear.

"What's going to happen now?" I heard Elyon ask Seth.

"Well, you can move back to Weston or…" Seth trailed off.

"Or what? Answer in full sentences please." She laughed and he gave a chuckle himself.

"Or, you can be my queen." He said softly. There was perfect silence and then a creak of the hospital bed. I heard Elyon gasp loudly, enough that I probably could have been down the hallway and still would have heard.

"Will you marry me, Elyon?"

Now I gasped, my breath caught and I couldn't breathe.

"Yes, yes, yes!" cheered Elyon. My legs wobbled and I felt an unconsciousness wave swoop over me.

I felt tears well in my eyes and I whispered *what's happening to me?*

Why was I crying? Shouldn't I have been happy for my sister? But I wasn't. I was angry. I didn't have anyone like that to love. Sure Darren loved me but Fates words imprinted on my mind and I was questioning myself *did I love* him *back?*

I re-entered the waiting room and shape-shifted my face to not show the tears.

"We shall leave now, apprentice." Fate said standing up from her chair and leaving the room. I followed her but at the door I looked back, though all I saw was an empty waiting room.

"Sorry, Elyon. I don't know you and…"

I sighed and pushed open the doors.

"You don't know me."

End of Book 1